Nicholas Patrick Wiseman

Dramas

The witch of Rosenburg

Nicholas Patrick Wiseman

Dramas
The witch of Rosenburg

ISBN/EAN: 9783337342043

Printed in Europe, USA, Canada, Australia, Japan

Cover: Foto ©Andreas Hilbeck / pixelio.de

More available books at **www.hansebooks.com**

DRAMAS:

THE WITCH OF ROSENBURG.

THE HIDDEN GEM.

BY

H. E. CARDINAL WISEMAN.

―――――――

A. M. D. G.

THE

WITCH OF ROSENBURG.

A

DRAMA IN THREE ACTS.

COMPOSED FOR THE CHILDREN OF

ST. LEO'S CONVENT, CARLOW, 1864.

BY

HIS EMINENCE CARDINAL WISEMAN,

ARCHBISHOP OF WESTMINSTER.

NEW YORK:

P O'SHEA, PUBLISHER,

45 WARREN STREET.

The Witch of Rosenburg,

A

DRAMA IN THREE ACTS.

This is the first and only manuscript of the Drama written by the Author, and forwarded to St. Leo's Convent, with his Blessing, and a request for prayers.

N. C. W.

London, November 15, 1864.

My Dear Cousin and Daughter in Christ:

It has pleased Almighty God to afflict me again with ill ness, and I write from my bed.

Many thanks for your kind letter on St. Nicholas' day; soon after this letter you will receive a small box, addressed to the Rev. Mother, from me; it is intended for the Community, and contains a little Christmas Present, of things from the Tyrol, not indeed of much value.

But my special desire is that it be opened at recreation in presence of all the Community, and you will let me know if they like it.

Prayers if you please—to-day is the anniversary of your foundation.

Your affectionate Father in Christ,

N. CARD. WISEMAN.

DRAMATIS PERSONÆ.

COUNTESS ANNA VON ROSENBURG, living in the Castle near.
BERTHA, her confidential maid.
LOTTE (Charlotte*), Schoolmistress in the village.
GRETCHEN (Margaret†), her friend.
FRAU PLUMPER, the Burgomaster's wife.
FRAU SEMMEL, the Baker's wife.
FRAU ZUCKER, the Grocer's wife.
THEIR THREE CHILDREN, and other girls.

The Scene is in a mountain village in the Tyrol.

[The opening Scene may be changed into a wood by having merely a curtain to fall before the image in the garden, as described in Scene I.]

The costumes as herewith sent, for the peasant women and girls.

Lotte in a simple dark gown and white apron, with a small cap, as a stranger, not in costume.

The *Countess* in more ordinary lady's dress, with white body and sleeves, and large hat with riband, &c.

Bertha the same, plainer, and wide brimmed straw hat.

N. B.—The colors in different parts of peasants' dresses may be varied—red being preferred.

* Karlotte—Lotte—Lotchen.
† Margarette—Greta—Gretchen.
The termination in *shon* is the more familiar and affectionate.

THE PROLOGUE.

If writing verse were but a poet's work,
I certainly should try this job to shirk;
But I have no resource; I fain must go it,
Though I shall thereby prove, I am no poet:
My orders are explicit;—write a play,
"Prologue and Epilogue,"—I must obey;
And so would you, if such a summons came,
So gently breathed, in dear St. Leo's name:
The purpose of a Prologue chiefly is,
To tell the moral bearing of the piece.
Now, my wish is—the youthful to remind,
Always to be considerate and kind,
Not to judge rashly—nor defects to spy,
But estimate with heart, as well as eye:
Not to despise, in pride of early strength,
Those whom, of days, God blesses with the length,
Though they may dim the eye, and curve the frame.
To be hand to the maimed, foot to the lame:
Seeking of age the pains thus to assuage;
To earn themselves, one day, a painless age.

Thus far our poet,—now it is *our* turn;
If it be his to teach,—'tis ours to learn:
May we, through life, to practise, never fail,
The lessons taught us in this simple tale!
Fearless to be, in innocence's cause,
Heedless alike of censure or applause;
So let us make of common plans reversal,
And treat what we shall act as a rehearsal;
What here is fiction—later will be fact.—
To-day we *practice*, what through life we hope to *act*.

THE WITCH OF ROSENBURG.

PART I.

SCENE I.—*A garden, in the centre of the background a statue of our Lady on a pedestal. In front six children, each holding a wreath of flowers, three on each side, in lines diverging from the statue towards the front,* LOTTE *in plain dark robe beside the image.*

LOTTE *and* CHILDREN.

CHORUS OF CHILDREN.

[Air, the Tyrolese Song of Liberty.—*Moore.*]

I.

Joyfully Mary's glories singing,
  Joyfully oh! joyfully oh!
Come we loving tribute bringing,
  Joyfully oh! joyfully oh!
Mist-clad echoes wake on the mountain,
Drown the roaring dash from the fountain:
  With her name above them ringing,
  Joyfully oh! joyfully oh!
Joyfully, joyfully, joyfully, joyfully, joyfully,
    joyfully oh!
  Joyfully oh! joyfully oh!

II.

Lovingly on her footsteps pressing,
        Lovingly oh! lovingly oh!
Let us gain her love and blessing,
        Lovingly oh! lovingly oh!
Mary be the star on us shining,
Whether life be fresh or declining,
    Her sweet smile our hearts caressing,
        Lovingly oh! lovingly oh!
Lovingly, lovingly, lovingly, lovingly, lovingly,
            lovingly oh!
        Lovingly oh! lovingly oh!

III.

Happily round her image closing,
        Happily oh! happily oh!
Round her feet our gifts disposing,
        Happily oh! happily oh!
Nothing shall on earth our hearts sever,
Mary's children be sisters ever!
    On her tender heart reposing,
        Happily oh! happily oh!
Happily, happily, happily, happily, happily,
            happily oh!
        Happily oh! happily oh!

[*At the beginning of the third stanza, the children, holding their wreaths, move inwards, still singing. The two in front go slowly before the others to the foot of the image.* LOTTE *takes their wreaths from them, and hangs them, by small hooks on them, to an invisible string round the foot or top of the pedestal. They return to their places behind the others ; so the two next, and the two last.*

While this is going on, enters the COUNTESS ANNA, *disguised in a red cloak and hood, which completely covers her dress, and conceals her features. She is bent double, leaning on a crutched stick, and trembling, shaking her hands and head, as if palsied. She creeps up slowly, so that when the children have finished, and turn fairly round, she has reached the middle, and they see her.*

The children are terrified, and scream, "A witch ! a witch !" and run away in every direction.]

LOTTE. Stop, stop! Don't be so foolish.

CHILD. A witch! a hag!

LOTTE. Fear nothing; stay with me, dear children.

CHILD. A witch! a witch!

[*Exeunt Children.*

SCENE II.—LOTTE *and* ANNA

ANNA. What is the matter? What is the meaning of this confusion?

LOTTE. Oh, nothing. Your sudden entrance startled the poor children, and they ran away. They will no doubt return again.

ANNA. Were they afraid of me, then?

2

LOTTE. You know these children of the mountains are inclined to be carried away by foolish terrors. But it will be my care to remove them to the utmost.

ANNA. I understand you. I heard their cries: they believe me to be a witch. Do you take me for one?

LOTTE. Oh no, no. I have no such fears.

ANNA. Are you not from this country? Your dress seems foreign.

LOTTE. No: I came from afar, and have only been here a few months.

ANNA. And you do not shrink from a poor old thing like me?

LOTTE. [aside. What a sweet voice she has for one so old!] Why should I? Am I not poor too?

ANNA. Yes; but you are young, and I am old and decrepit.

LOTTE. Then so much the more you need assistance from the young.

ANNA. And have you no repugnance to an ugly old hag, as the children called me?

LOTTE. [laughing.] Poor things! Do they not pray daily that their parents should enjoy a long life; and is not decrepitude, or palsy, or, if you please, ugliness, almost a condition of their prayers being heard?

ANNA. Then you fear no mischance from me? You do not believe me to be spiteful, or mischievous, or likely to harm you?

LOTTE. No, my good grandame, I fear not man.

ANNA. No! Then have you *no* fear?

LOTTE. Yes, I have a twofold fear, but very different in their characters.

ANNA. What are they?

LOTTE. I fear God, and I fear sin: the one with love, the other with abhorrence.

ANNA. Happy the mother that owns such a child! [*Lotte bursts into tears.*] What is the matter, child? Have I hurt your feelings? [*Soothingly.*] Have you suffered misfortune?

LOTTE. I have no mother! I am a poor orphan; a friendless wanderer upon earth. No, not friendless. [*Pointing upwards.*] I have a Father there.

ANNA. O that I could be a mother to you on earth! But what can a poor helpless creature like me do for any one?

LOTTE. Much, very much.

ANNA. What?

LOTTE. Give the young the merit of helping you. [*Puts a gold coin into Anna's hand, who takes it.*]

ANNA. Thank you a thousand times. [*Looks at it intently.*] But gold! Where got you this?

You ill can spare it.   It is pierced and has been
worn. [*Much agitated.*] Where has it been ?

LOTTE. It was my poor mother's, and my father's
before her.   I have no other, and feel ashamed
to wear it or keep it when I see one before me
in greater need than myself.

ANNA. But you are poor yourself.

LOTTE. Yet young and strong, and can work for
my bread.   The little salary for my schooling,
my knitting and sewing, give me enough to live
on.

ANNA. [*moved.*] Child, God will bless you for
your charity—yes, your fearless charity to a
poor helpless old stranger.   But I must leave
you.

LOTTE. Will you not come and rest in my poor
cottage ?   It is hard by.

ANNA. No, thank you ; you have made me richer
than I have been this many a day.   Will you
give me your arm to the high road, and then I
will totter along.

[LOTTE *gives* ANNA *her arm, and leads her out, when they come
to the side,* ANNA *stops.*]

ANNA. What were you doing when I came in
here ?

LOTTE. The children were practising for a village
festival a song which I had composed and put
to a popular air for them.

ANNA. And I appeared like a hawk amongst your chicks, and frightened them away. I fear I have done you mischief, and yet you have been kind to me, and shown no anger.

LOTTE. [*laughing cheerfully.*] How could I have acted otherwise? I should not have been a Christian else.

ANNA. Where did you acquire these principles—aye, and your accomplishments? Poor children do not learn to compose songs, and put them to music.

LOTTE. My dear mother, before her death, secured to me the best education in St. Leo's Convent, near the place of my birth; it was my only inheritance, and my best.

ANNA. And was it from her you inherited your courage?

LOTTE. My father, whom I never knew, was an officer of high rank. If there is anything in it I may owe it to him.

ANNA. [*starting.*] An officer! Well, adieu. God bless you.

LOTTE. Good bye, my good old dame. [*Leads her out and then returns.*]

2*

SCENE III.—LOTTE *alone.*

LOTTE. Poor thing! how will she ever get home without help? I wonder where her home is. She seemed to be a stranger to the children. Poor children, too, I may well say. That they should have been frightened away by a poor harmless old woman—taking her for a witch. No doubt their parents will give them a good lesson, perhaps chastise them, for being so weak and silly. In the meantime, their little festival has been spoiled.

How thankful I ought to be that a good education has made me feel so differently, and only compassionately towards the miserable. Suffering ourselves is a great lesson.

But what a mystery my own poor little life is to myself.

Who and what was my father? My mother, who died so young, could only tell me that he was a noble officer in garrison, in the distant province where I was born, and married her, a poor peasant; but before he could make his marriage known to his family, was killed in quelling a riot.

Here are his precious relics. [*Taking them from her bosom.*] This is his portrait. [*Kiss-*

ing it and replacing it.] This is the invaluable document which attests his marriage; this his last letter, unfinished and without his name, but stained with his blood.

But of what use are these papers to me, who know not where to look for his family? I have wandered thus far, and must rest contented to end my days as schoolmistress at Rosenburg. [*Hears some one coming, and hastily puts back the papers.*]

SCENE IV.—LOTTE *and* GRETCHEN.

GRETCHEN. [*rushing in, singing* To-le-ra-la, *or some such cadence.*] What, dear Lotchen, alone? I thought some of your children would be here. Have they all run away? What has been the matter?

LOTTE. Oh, nothing. Have *you* heard or seen anything?

GRET. Heard or seen anything? I should think so. Both. I never saw such a regular *hullabaloo* in our quiet village.

First, I met the children running in, screaming, some tumbling over and crying. Among these was little Plumper, the tailor's—that is, the Burgomaster's—child [*sarcastically*], who fell with a great crash at her father's door. Everybody came out in a terrible state, and questioned the children, who at first could give no account of their panic. At last they told an incoherent story of a witch having appeared, nobody knew how, at the school, and attacked them with a stick; that she had two eyes like coals, and a beard and hair like adders; and so they ran away. So I thought I would come and learn the truth.

LOTTE. Really, Gretchen, I can hardly help laughing—only I fear the poor children may have really suffered.

GRET. Pooh, pooh, Lotchen, they will be no worse after they have each had a cup of tea, or a thump on the back, according to the disposition of their parents. But what is it all about?

LOTTE. The fact is that a poor old palsied woman, in a red cloak, made a sudden appearance here, while the children were rehearsing my little hymn, when they took wing like a flock of starlings. The poor woman said not a word, and I, who remained, never saw her face. She was bent double, and kept her hood low down.

GRET. [*shaking her head gravely.*] Do you know, Lotchen, that I fear I should have run away too. An old woman, doubled down, in a red cloak, and wagging her head! no, I could hardly have stood it. Ah, now, don't laugh at me. You are a scholar, and I am only a poor orphan, that can only knit and sew, and scarcely read. But really, if all that does not make a witch, I don't know what does.

LOTTE. Why, my dear Gretchen, nothing does.

GRET. Nonsense, now. You don't mean that.

LOTTE. Well, we will talk it over. In the meantime——

GRET. Why, look out for squalls. You must come away.

LOTTE. What for?

GRET. Because, before I came up the hill here, I saw a solemn conclave being held in the square by Frau Plumper, who was very red, Frau Zucker, who was very pale, and Frau Semmel, who was very blue; and I'm sure there was mischief brewing among them. They were pointing this way. So as Frau Plumper went in to get her walking shoes, being always in slippers, and I know she can only go gingerly up hill, I ran straight up to warn you.

LOTTE. I am ready to face them, and speak the truth to them.

GRET. They will not listen to you. So come with me to the little chapel in the forest, and I will

come back and let you know when the coast is
clear.

[*She takes* LOTTE'S *arm, and leads her away, singing, as in
the opening chorus :*]

" Nothing shall on earth our hearts sever,
Mary's orphans be sisters ever."   [*Exeunt.*

SCENE V.—*Enter* PLUMPER, SEMMEL *and* ZUCKER.

PLUMPER. [*looking about and out of breath.*] So
she is gone, is she?   A nice thing, isn't she, to
make us come up all this hill, on purpose to see
her, and she to get out of the way?   [*Puffing.*]

SEM. Just like her.   But what is to be done?

ZUCK. The probability is that she went off with
the witch.   She seemed very familiar, as my
little Sophia told me, having had courage to
look once behind her, to pick up her shoe,
which, I am sorry to say, she ripped open on a
stone.

SEM. Ah, to be sure.   The children said she had
a stick.   What sort of stick was it, I wonder?

ZUCK. Of course, as she was a witch, it must have
been a broomstick.

SEM. No doubt.   Indeed, I think some of the
dear children said that it was a broomstick,
with the broom end upwards, on which she
leaned all her weight.   She could not have
leaned so on the top.

PLUMP. It seems all plain now. To-night is the Walpurgis night, when all the witches meet in the Karz mountains, to which they ride through the air. Witches are always skinny, you know, and this wicked Lotte is not stout, so probably one broomstick did for both.

SEM. How else could the witch have got away?

PLUMP. Exactly. You know that at my request my man Karl, that is the Burgomaster, who never refuses me anything reasonable, and of course I never ask for anything else, sent off Hans and Fritz, his two most nimble journeymen, in pursuit—one up, one down the road. Hans, who, though thin in body and long in legs, is very courageous, ran much farther than it was possible for so old, doubled, and palsied a creature to have got. Yet he met nobody except the Countess, who was hurrying before him to her carriage, with Bertha, carrying a large bundle, which he believed to be a blanket for some poor person.

So, nothing daunted, he asked her boldly if she had seen or passed a witch on the road.

ZUCK. And what did she answer? She must have been much alarmed.

PLUMP. Not at all. As he told me when he called me aside on our way up here, she only smiled and said, "My good friend, how am I to tell a witch from anybody else?"

SEM. Of course, he had no difficulty in answering that.

PLUMP. Oh, as he described her: red cloak, bent double, shaking, &c.

SEM. What did she say then?

PLUMP. Why she actually laughed out, and so did Mam'selle Bertha.   Then the Countess replied: "I assure you, we have neither *passed* nor *met* any one such as you describe."

ZUCK. All this comes of your fine education, now-a-days, which makes people laugh at what their forefathers believed.

PLUMP. Yes; Hans, who is a very mild and right-thinking youth, though slender, said he was rather hurt by such levity.   However, though she has escaped this time, she will not the next.

Karl, that is the Burgomaster, will have her looked after, and brought to *benign* punishment.

SEM. And what would that be?

PLUMP. Well, I believe, strictly speaking, it would be burning to death.

ZUCK. Oh, shocking! terrible!   That would never do.   I like a bonfire very much; but I own I could not look at one, with even a wicked witch inside of it.

PLUMP. Well, then, there is a milder treatment by water.

ZUCK. How is that?

PLUMP. By ducking her in a pond.

SEM. Well, that *is* better; but I should be sorry to go even so far. Suppose, therefore, that we leave matters of law to the men, and look to our own affairs. Do you think the witch has done any harm so far?

PLUMP. I hope not. For my part, when my little pet came running in like a frightened dove, I did not for a moment lose my presence of mind. Poor Karl, that is the Burgomaster, was measuring a new customer for a jacket, and dropped his measure in his fright, and let the shears fall on his foot. But I immediately seized the child, and gave her a good shaking, to bring her back to her senses. When she had told me about the witch, I added a few smart whacks between the shoulders, to make her cough, in case she had swallowed a lot of crooked pins. Then I looked and saw she did not squint with the other eye, and that her feet were not more turned in than they were before, poor child! so I was satisfied.

ZUCK. What a good mother you are, Frau Plump-er; I never thought of any of these remedies.

3

SEM. Nor I. But now what is to be done about that sly creature Lotte?

PLUMP. Why certainly—[*A singing* Tol-la-rol *is heard.*] There is that silly Gretchen coming. She will tell us where she is to be found.

[*Enter* GRETCHEN, *tripping in.*]

SCENE VI.—*The same and* GRETCHEN.

GRET. [*astonished.*] I beg pardon, ladies; you here? What has happened to bring you up here?

PLUMP. Why, have you not heard?

GRET. [*aside.*] I don't choose to have heard. [*Aloud.*] Pray tell me.

PLUMP. Surely you know that a witch has been here, and that your friend Lotte is deeply involved in her sudden disappearance.

GRET. Indeed; how?

ZUCK. Yes, indeed. The witch and Lotte vanished at the same time; and as no one can doubt as to *how* the one travelled, there is strong suspicion that Lotte went by the same conveyance.

GRET. And what is that?

SEM. Don't affect ignorance. You know very well.

GRET. Then was that person whom I saw with Lotte in the wood, certainly the witch?

ALL. [*eagerly rushing forward.*] *Most* certainly. Do tell us all you have seen.

PLUMP. What was her height?

GRET. About my own.

ZUCK. Hideously ugly?

GRET. Not more than I am.

SEM. In a red cloak?

GRET. No: in a peasant's ordinary dress.

PLUMP. Then it is plain the witch had transformed herself into——

GRET. Me!

ALL. [*indignantly.*] How! are you the witch in the form of Gretchen?

PLUMP. If so, heaven be 'twixt us and harm. Avaunt, avaunt you!

GRET. [*laughing immoderately.*] No, no, no, I am only Gretchen, the poor orphan girl.

[*The others come forward, having shrunk away, repeating,* Avaunt, you, you witch !]

ZUCK. How dare you frighten honest people by pretending to be a witch?

GRET. I? I never did any such thing. *I* was the person with whom Lotte went away into the wood. So if it was the witch that went away with her, I must be, madam, the hexe.*

* Witch.

But see, here poor Lotchen herself comes, impatient, no doubt, for my return according to promise.

SCENE VII.—*The same and* LOTTE.

LOTTE. My dear Gretchen, I got anxious to see you return, so I came after you. Ladies, good morning! To what do I owe the pleasure of this unexpected visit?

PLUMP. To a previous visit, from a perhaps more welcome guest.

LOTTE. Indeed! Pray, from whom? For surely there are none in the village for whom I ought to feel, or do feel, more regard than the ladies who so kindly patronize me, and entrust me with the education of their children.

PLUMP. Yes, and a pretty return *we* have; and a nice education *they* get.

LOTTE. How, ma'am? I own I am very deficient, but I trust I do my best.

ZUCK. I suppose by introducing them to such company as nearly frightened them to death this morning.

LOTTE. How could I help that poor old creature coming inside the gate, to see and hear those pretty children?

SEM. Yes, very likely, indeed. As if she was
not your friend, the horrid thing! You seemed
very familiar with her.

LOTTE. Not more than I hope always to be with
any distressed object of compassion.

PLUMP. Hear her, hear her! A witch is to her
an object of compassion.

GRET. Gently, gently, mother Plumper, you have
no proof that it was a witch.

PLUMP. No proof! A hideous, crooked hag

GRET. Who saw her face?

LOTTE. Certainly, *I* did not.

GRET. Did any of the children? Did yours?

PLUMP. Well, I don't think she did.

GRET. Or yours?

ZUCK. She couldn't on account of the hood.

GRET. Or yours?

SEM. She never said she did.

GRET. Then on whose authority do you report
her supreme ugliness?

PLUMP. What stuff! [*Huffed.*] As if it was possible that a witch should be otherwise than
hideous.

GRET. Oh, now I see. She was a witch because
she was ugly, and she was ugly because she was
a witch. [*Curtseying.*]

PLUMP. Did you ever hear such impudence?

3*

LOTTE. Do not be angry, ma'am, with poor Gretchen; after all, she only spoke the truth.

ZUCK. You had better mind your own affairs;
you have plenty to think for yourself. Do you
think I will ever send my children again to be
taught by one who makes light of charmers and
soothsayers?

LOTTE. I know what penalty your withdrawal of
your children will inflict on me. In the name
of justice, then, answer me, before I am con-
demned. [*With dignity.*] Tell me, then, Dame
Zucker, since I came here, three months ago,
have your children gone back, or have they ad-
vanced? Have they applied more or less?
Have they learnt more and better than previ-
ously? Have you praised or blamed their mistress and their education? You hesitate; come,
answer, for the sake of justice and truth to the
heavens above.

ZUCK. [*abashed.*] Well, I own that till to-day,
when my dear little Sophia came running in
with her shoe ripped up, I have never had cause
to complain.

LOTTE. And you, Frau Semmel, do you intend to
remove your child?

'SEM. Most certainly. I would not think of leaving her with the friend of conjurers and fortune-
tellers.

LOTTE. Be it so; but I conjure you to answer me
in all sincerity : Since your daughter has been
under my care, has she become more or less
docile, obedient, cheerful ? Has she diminished
in affection to you and her family; or has she
been morose, ill-tempered and selfish ? Speak
out the truth, and heaven will bless you.

SEM. Well, I must own that she is, in all these
respects, wonderfully changed for the better, in
the last three months.

LOTTE. Thank you; this is indeed a consolation.
And now, Madam Plumper, upon whom I know
my fate depends, more than on any one else,
tell me if your child has of late become more
serious and steady, more truthful, more recol-
lected, more watchful to correct her failings—in
fine, more religious, edifying and devout, since,
than before she came under my tuition?

PLUMP. Oh, I admit all this. Certainly she is
most remarkably improved since you came.
But how am I to know that all this does not
come from magical arts and charms? I will
run no risk. We three are patronesses of the
school, and it cannot last one day after we with-
draw our protection. We can easily find another
mistress.

GRET. [*curtseying.*] Pray, ma'am, take me; I can

teach your children the clever use of the knitting-needles and spinning wheel, to which they had better return, since you do not seem to value dear Lotchen's learning and the moral good she has taught your children.

LOTTE. Peace, dear Gretchen. Ladies, I own I was not prepared for this sudden close of my occupation here. After much wandering and much suffering, Providence seemed to have guided my footsteps here. I hoped that, in my humble sphere, I was doing my best to discharge my duties, and not unsuccessfully. I looked forward to years of peace in contented poverty. I love the children of Rosenburg, and they appeared to love me. I looked forward to see them grow up round me, not so much patronesses as friends; and then to sleep among them in the "dear God's field," with my little wooden cross over me, on which some of them would hang, sometimes, a garland, with the simple inscription, "Lotte, the Schoolmistress."

ZUCK. [moved.] Really, Frau Plumper, perhaps, you know——

SEM. You know it may have all been an unfortunate accident.

PLUMP. No such thing. We should be disgraced

if we tolerated it. What would the people of
Blum and Spondel and Stein say of Rosenburg,
if they heard it? No, Miss Lotte, go you
must. Only one thing I beg: go away altogether, and do not remain in our neighborhood,
to draw away our children.

LOTTE. Madam, I will obey you so far as I acknowledge your authority; but must decline to
do so further. I am alone in the world; I have
no roof over my head when I leave the school-
house.

GRET. Yes, yes; you have one in my garret: you
shall share all with me. " Mary's orphans ever
sisters be."

LOTTE. No, dear Gretchen, it cannot be; I will
honestly earn my own bread, and I will seek it
where I may still see my dear little ones, and
pray in our sweet church.

GRET. But where will you obtain occupation?

LOTTE. Dear friend, you know that the orphan is
not fatherless. Never yet have I been forsaken
in my many wanderings. I have heard much
of the unbounded kindness and charity of the
Countess Anna: perhaps she will give me some
little to do while I look about me.

GRET. [aside.] I will take that hint, and see what
I can do. [Aloud.] Yes, I think that good and

noble lady will take a more generous view of
your case than these good village dames.

PLUMP. [*aloud and indignant.*] It shall be my
care, miss, to inform the Countess of all that
has happened ; and she is too good a Christian
to countenance witchcraft and sorcery. So put
no hopes there, but leave at once, and let us
never see you again.

CHORUS.

[PLUMPER, SEMMEL *and* ZUCKER.]

Wicked girl, begone, begone ;
    Go : avaunt, thou witch's friend !
Henceforth, of our children, none
    Thy false teaching shall attend.

[GRETCHEN *is in tears : on one side with* ZUCKER, *the other two
on the other.   Towards the end,* LOTTE, *who is in the middle,
looking upwards, with her hands clasped, throws out her arms,
still with her eyes to heaven, when the curtain drops.*]

END OF PART I.

ACT II.

SCENE I.—*A forest;* LOTTE *and* GRETCHEN *discovered, seated on a low rock or stone,* GRETCHEN *with her right hand covering her eyes, and her left in* LOTTE'S *right, sobbing.*

LOTTE *and* GRETCHEN.

LOTTE. Courage, my dear sister, courage! Console yourself! [*Gret. sobs.*] Why really one would think that *you* are the one who is driven out homeless and shelterless, and not I.

GRET. And so I am equally with you. [*They rise.*]

LOTTE. How, dearest?

GRET. Because I am determined to share your fate altogether. Either you come home with me and share my garret and my crust, or I remain with you in the forest till you have found a home.

LOTTE. No, my dear child, this cannot be. It is unreasonable and unkind.

GRET. Why so? Why at least unkind?

LOTTE. Because if *Providence*, in its wisdom, has driven me abroad, a poor wanderer, it is unreasonable for *man* to do the same to another, without having the same wisdom; and it is unkind in him to double that trial which God has inflicted.

GRET. And should *I* do that?

LOTTE. Certainly, dearest sister; to see you suffer as much as myself would be to double my measure of unhappiness. So let me bear my burden alone, till better days. They will soon come.

GRET. Then come and share my humble roof and fare.

LOTTE. That, too, is quite impossible.

GRET. Why?

LOTTE. Imagine what a most unpleasant position it would be for all parties, for those ladies and myself to be meeting every minute, face to face, and either to be passing one another cold and hard, or paying insincere courtesies.

GRET. Well, I have no doubt, Lotchen, that *you* do not speak this way through pride. But if I had been treated as abominably as you have, *my* spirit would be up, and I should delight in tossing up my head like a young heifer every time I passed those great ladies. However, never mind, won't *I* do so for you!

LOTTE. No, my dear Gretchen, don't do any such thing. Listen to me. For three months I have been doing my best to inculcate on the neglected village children the duty of docile obedience to their parents. I have particularly

taught them to respect their judgment, and not
to set their own above it, nor to consider them
stupid or ignorant, nor ordinarily in the wrong.

GRET. Well, Lotchen, I own you are cleverer
than I thought you, if you have made them
think *that*.

LOTTE. Well, never mind. The children, I know,
love me; and what a pretty finish I should put
to all my teaching were I now so to act as to
force them by my presence to one of these
alternatives: either to take part with their
parents, and so cease to love me, or to take my
side, and so through me lose that filial deference
which I have so strongly impressed on them.

GRET. [*seizing Lotte's hand.*] Oh, my darling
Lotchen, how good and considerate you are!

LOTTE. Dear Gretchen, the memory of children,
while such, is very short. I would rather slip
gradually out of their minds, with a slowly
lingering love, than be remembered as the fire-
brand that kindled enmities in households.
And then there is a higher consideration still.

GRET. What can that be?

LOTTE. I have been ever endeavoring to instil
into those tender minds never to retain malice,
or worse, a grudge, still less display one. In
their little childish quarrels, I have tried to

4

make them feel that the one who considered, or knew herself right, should be the first to give way and make it up, on the ground that she could best afford to be generous. What will all my past teaching be worth if now, believing myself right, I show stubbornness and resentment?

On the other hand, how happy ought I to feel, and even thankful, that an opportunity has been afforded me of teaching by example the most difficult of my lessons. Perhaps my heavy trial has been sent to me on purpose.

GRET. Dear good Lotchen, you are right. Indeed you are sure to be right, while I, a poor clumsy country girl, am sure to be wrong. *You* ought to have been born a princess.

LOTTE. Hush, hush, Gretchen; no murmuring, please.

GRET. However, you do not want to leave the neighborhood?

LOTTE. No; as I have said, I have an impression that I may yet do some good here, and perhaps from time to time catch a glimpse of my dear children, without giving offence.

GRET. And you would not refuse occupation from our noble lady?

LOTTE. Certainly not; I have heard so much of

her kindness. But how approach her? I have never spoken to her.

GRET. Leave that to me. Go and rest again in the little chapel for a short time, and when you are tired come back here.

[*Leads her away, then returns.*

SCENE II.—GRETCHEN *and* BERTHA

GRET. So now, Gretchen, let us see what your little head is fit for. It is yet early in the day, and I shall be but a poor manager if dear Lotchen sleeps in the woods to-night. Everybody is kind to me about here, and there is hardly a cottage that will not take her in for me; and gratis, too, for I fear we have neither of us much to pay a lodging with. By the by, the poor thing has eaten nothing; how shall I manage that? Oh, here comes one that will help me.

[*Enter* BERTHA.]

BERTHA. Good day, Gretchen.

GRET. Good day, Mam'selle Bertha. You are the very person I wanted most to see.

BER. How fortunate! But tell me, was that Lotte, the village schoolmistress, that you parted with just now?

GRET. The village schoolmistress that was.

BER. How! not that *is* now?

GRET. That was a few hours ago, but that has been summarily dismissed and sent out a poor lonely outcast on the world.   Poor child!

BER. By whom?

GRET. By the great dames of Rosenburg, Madam Plumper & Co.

BER. What for?

GRET. For a great crime, no doubt.   For nothing less than harboring and abetting, as I have heard Herr Papickschonntzer, the notary, call it, a witch.

BER. A witch!

GRET. Yes; a witch in a red cloak.   [*Bertha laughs violently.*]   Yes, *you* may laugh, who have the best of the castle up there.   But it is no laughing matter to poor Lotchen [*hurt*], who may have to pass the night with the wolves in the forest; for she won't share my lodging, out of pure delicacy.

BER. Pardon me, dear Gretchen; I assure you I was laughing at anything but poor Lotte.   She shall not sleep in the wood.   I will see to that.   But tell me, do you know anything of her history?   You seem to be her only friend.   Does she make any mystery of her life?

GRET. Oh, dear, no. She is too simple for that. That she is a lady born I have no doubt: everything about her, except her dress, shows that.

BER. Then what account does she give of herself?

GRET. She is incapable of boasting. but she has told *me* several things.

BER. She was an officer's child, was she not?

GRET. [*surprised.*] Who told you *that?*

BER. Oh, I heard it somewhere.

GRET. Well, that *is* strange. But it is true. Her father seems to have been killed in an engagement soon after his marriage with a peasant girl, her mother, who died while she was yet young, leaving means to educate her. She wandered in search of her family, till, broken down with fatigue and disappointment, she accepted her late office.

BER. But perhaps this history may be the result of an illusion without proof.

GRET. Illusion, Miss Bertha! Lotte is incapable of illusion. She has every proof in papers carefully preserved. Unfortunately her father's name is torn out of the certificate of marriage, except his title of Count Ludwig——

BER. [*astonished.*] Count Ludwig?

GRET. Yes; but then she has a miniature of him round her neck, which it would be impossible

not to recognize as the portrait of Lotchen's
father.

BER. [*agitated.*] Would it be possible to see these
various objects?

GRET. When once she is quietly in some home,
however humble, she will refuse you nothing.
You do not know her yet, as I do; you will,
perhaps, one day.

BER. Thanks, Gretchen, I must go to procure her
shelter.   But, one moment more, I fear she may
be in want of food.   Is she in distress?

GRET. Well, I doubt if she has taken anything
to-day.   She should want for nothing that I
might have to give.   But unfortunately I live
by my daily toil, and to-day I have earned
nothing.   As for poor Lotchen, I suspect her
purse is as empty as mine.

BER. [*taking out her purse.*] I thought she was
better off.   She gave a gold piece very lately to
a poor person.   It seemed to have been worn
as a keepsake; and so it has come into my
hands.

GRET. Dear, unselfish soul! She must have parted
with one of the proofs of her birth in charity!
It was a coin with a saint's figure on it, left her
as father's.   No: she would give her heart
away to a poor person.   But if she parted with

that coin, depend upon it she had not a penny left.

BER. [*giving her money.*] Go, good Gretchen; run and bring your admirable friend some nourishment as quickly as possible.

GRET. God bless you, Mam'selle Bertha. Perhaps, however, I had better go round, and tell Lotte not to come here till I fetch her. She might be startled at finding you instead of me.

BER. That is quite right. And pray, Gretchen, say nothing about the Countess to her—you must for the present deal with me.

[*Exit Gretchen.*

SCENE III.—BERTHA *and* COUNTESS ANNA.

ANNA. My true Bertha, have you made anything out of the doings in the village?

BER. Yes, all. And, my kind mistress, I have much to tell you, which will, I think, astonish you.

ANNA. But first let me know something about this poor girl whom you know I have taken an almost foolish fancy for.

BER. No, Madam, not foolish; quite the contrary. She is worthy of all your patronage, and perhaps more.

Anna. In what way?

Ber. She seems, by all account, not merely a well-educated girl, but of a most refined and virtuous mind, religious, charitable, and unselfish in the highest degree.

Anna. Of the last, I think we have evidence in that gold piece which I put into your hands to learn the history of. Have you made it out?

Ber. I think I have. But I must tell you about it more at leisure, as it must be talked of with other things. For the present, there is something still more urgent.

Anna. What is that?

Ber. That poor Lotte is wandering here in the forest, without a roof for the night or bread for the day.

Anna. Is that possible? Did those village ladies turn her adrift without any compensation? Had she no little savings about her?

Ber. Not a farthing. In giving that gold piece to the witch that you know something of, which is now in my hands, she gave away her last coin. In fact she gives away everything.

Anna. [moved and serious.] And yet, Bertha, we consider ourselves charitable and expect lavish thanks when we drop the overflow of our purses on the heads of the poor. Surely, it is the truest charity when the cup of cold water which was just rising to the lips of the weary poor is turned aside and placed between those of one poorer and thirstier. Not only the widow's copper mites, but this orphan's golden token, will one day rise in judgment against us. But we are losing time about her.

BER. I hope not. I have sent her trusty and loving friend Gretchen to provide her refreshments at once. A lodging is the next thing.

ANNA. Oh, that is easily done. There is poor Elizabeth, whose son is gone from home, and who keeps her cottage so neat, who will gladly let her empty room.

BER. Nothing could be better. I will see to all arrangements You had better not appear in the matter. I will settle it with Gretchen.

ANNA. Do, please. When you have told me all you know about her, and I satisfy myself of the truth of her history, it will be time enough for me to see her. If she be truly an officer's daughter, which may account for that coin having got into her hands, we can easily provide for her in a manner more befitting her rank. Should it turn out to be a mistake, for deceit is not to be thought of here, it will have spared

her some pain and mortification not to have
seen me.

BER. True indeed, and most delicate on your part.
But here comes Gretchen.

SCENE IV.—*The same and* GRETCHEN.

BER. Well, Gretchen, is all right? You have
been very quick.

GRET. [*respectfully curtseying to the Countess.*]
Yes, I fortunately met a person in the forest
selling what I wanted, and took it to Lotte.
Poor thing, she is most grateful. Does the
Countess know her case?

ANNA. Yes, indeed; and I have already given
Bertha directions about her having a nice lodging prepared for her.

GRET. God bless you, Madam, for your kindness;
I said I was sure you would not let her suffer
want or distress.

ANNA. Yet what have I done compared with what
you have? You, a poor girl yourself, devoting
yourself to your friend.

GRET. Oh, it is nothing for me. But she will be
coming here just now by appointment, and perhaps, Ma'am, you would not like being seen
with me by her.

ANNA. No, I think it is better not at present. Let us retire, and we will meet again.

BER. But Gretchen can tell you more of what we have to talk about than I. She had better come with us.

GRET. Willingly: Lotte is to wait here for me if I am gone.

SCENE V.—*As they are going out, enter on the other side, in the background,* CHILDREN (*six or more*), *with little baskets, singing as below, as they gather flowers dispersed;* LOTTE *also comes in, and stands apart. Neither she nor the children see the* COUNTESS, *&c., who pauses at the side.*

[*The same,* LOTTE, CHILDREN.]

ANNA. What a pretty sight! Let us stay a moment and watch it here apart.

CHILDREN. [*singing.*]—

CHORUS OF CHILDREN.

I.

Be 't ours in summer bowers
To pick our Lady's flowers;
Lilies, blue bells, and wild roses.

II.

'Tis good in wintry wood
To gather for the rood,
Beaded holly's prickly posies.

[They stand together.

1st CHILD. That is one of the many pretty songs
that dear Lotte taught us.

2ND CH. Dear Lotte! I wonder what has become
of her.

3RD CH. How I should like to see her again.

LOTTE. [*who has stolen in behind, unseen—aside.*]
Dear children, how I love them.

1st CH. How stupid it was of us this morning to
run away on account of that poor old woman in
red.

2ND CH. But she was a witch, wasn't she?

1st CH. Witch or no witch, we had no business
to run away while Lotchen was there.

2ND CH. Certainly, *she* would not stay a moment
with anything wicked.

3RD CH. No, nor run away from anything that
was not evil.

1st CH. I am so sorry to have acted so foolishly
and alarmed my parents.

3RD CH. And brought so much trouble on poor
dear Lotte. I have brought my bread and
some fruit from dinner for her, in case I should
meet her.

2ND CH. And I put my good mother's birthday
present, half a florin, in my pocket, to get her
a lodging somewhere.

ANNA. [*apart.*] See what a treasure these good ladies parted with in their mistress.

BER. How the children love her.

GRET. Love her! I should think so, indeed. And so will *you* love her one day, Madam, when you know her as well as we do. But perhaps not; her virtues are perhaps better suited and more congenial to us poor folks than to great ones, who know so much more.

ANNA. No, no. It is from the poor that the rich have generally to learn their virtues. But see, Lotte is stepping forward.

[LOTTE, *who has been watching and listening to the children with great emotion, unseen by them, rushes, much agitated, into the midst of them.*]

LOTTE. Children, my dear children!

CHILDREN. [*closing round her, clapping their hands, and seizing hers, cry out.*] Lotte, dear Lotchen! are you here? Oh, come home again. We will not run away again for any one.

LOTTE. My children, I cannot return, at least now. What a happiness it is to me to find that you still love me.

CHIL. Yes, indeed, we all love you.

LOTTE. If you love me, practise what I have always taught you: to love and obey your parents above all on earth. If your love to

5

them clash with your love for me, you know
which you must prefer. And you have sacred
duties towards them, but no longer any towards
me. Farewell, my children.

CHIL. But you only make us love you the more
by speaking thus.

[LOTTE *covers her face with her hands. The children make a
half circle round her, and sing.*]

CHORUS.

I.

Come back to us, Lotte good,
   Never seen in wayward mood,
   Gentle even with the rude:
Come back to us, mistress good.

II.

Come back for us, Lotte kind,
   To our failings ever blind,
   Forming heart as well as mind:
Come back for us, mistress kind.

III.

Come back with us, Lotte dear,
   Look on us and dry that tear,
   Children's love bids nought to fear:
Come back with us, mistress dear.

[*At the last verse the curtain drops.*]

END OF ACT II.

ACT III.

SCENE I.—*The School Garden.* BERTHA *and* GRETCHEN, *meeting from opposite sides.*]

BER. Well met, Gretchen, have you done all we agreed?

GRET. Yes. I have been to the boys' school, and find the men gathering there. What a feast is laid out for them! everything that they are most sure to like.

BER. Yes; Franz, the Countess' steward, understands all that perfectly, and takes a real pleasure in carrying out her kind purposes.

GRET. And I am sure you have done as much for the ladies' department.

BER. You have seen Lotte? She will come?

GRET. She will do anything she is desired. Of course it was a little painful to her to meet her late patronesses. But the moment she was told that the Countess wished it, she consented at once. She is so sweet, and then so grateful.

BER. And the Countess is so fond of her.

GRET. Then tell me, Mam'selle Bertha, why has she never sent for her, or gone to see her, as she does so many other poor people? I think Lotte must feel a little hurt; but she has never complained.

BER. You will know soon. You remember the Countess wished first to see her papers, which she has done—indeed, she has kept them.

GRET. And is she satisfied?

BER. Quite; they clearly make out her claim to be the orphan daughter of a distinguished officer, and the Countess proposes to provide for her as such.

GRET. Oh, how nice for dear Lotchen, and how good of the Countess! But how soon will this be made known?

BER. Now, immediately. Indeed, this is the main object of the feast. The Countess wishes to vindicate Lotte's honor and declare her position in the face of those who have so insulted and injured her.

GRET. How delightful! I must see this—won't I skip and jump!

BER. Take care, Gretchen, do not hurt their feelings more than is necessary. Come with me for a moment, then return to keep order among the children, especially when Lotte appears.

[*Exeunt.*

SCENE II.—*Enter the Children, except 2nd and 3rd*

1ST CHILD. We are not all here. Where are Barbara and Amelia?

2ND CH. [*skipping in.*] Here I am, and Amelia is coming.

1ST CH. What has kept you back?

2ND CH. We looked into the school-room. What a feast! We never had such a one before.

3RD CH. Oh, what a treat! [*Bounding forward.*] You should have stopped to see it.

1ST CH. No indeed; I am not going to be greedy, like you.

3RD CH. Greedy! it is indeed enough to make one greedy.

ALL. What is there? Do tell us. Never mind Bridget's airs.

3RD CH. Why, there are cakes, and jellies, and creams.

2ND CH. And all sorts of fruits from the castle garden.

3RD CH. Aye, and from the hot-houses, peaches, and heaps of grapes.

2ND CH. And there are two huge cherry tarts, each as big as one of the Countess' carriage hind wheels. I can't conceive where they were baked.

5*

3RD CH. And two plum cakes, the size of the front ones.

ALL. Oh, how nice!

[*Some rub their hands, some suck or smack their lips, and all dance about.*]

1ST CH. You need not be so excited. All the village is to come; and depend upon it we children, though the first come, will be the last served.

2ND CH. Oh, as to that, there is enough for three villages.

3RD CH. That is true. But, Barbara, if you had staid longer with me, you would have seen that there were things for us expressly, and not for our *betters*, as they like to call themselves on such occasions.

ALL. What was that?

3RD CH. Well, there were two baskets, immense ones, on one side, covered with napkins, and I could not resist the temptation to peep under.

1ST CH. For shame, Amelia. Don't you remember how Lotte used to tell us never to try to see anything that was shut up or covered, and teach us to repress our curiosity?

2ND CH. Very true, but now that she *has* looked, she may as well tell us what the baskets contained.

3RD CH. Well, the first was full of sugar plums, comfits, and such things, which could only be intended for us.

1ST CH. Indeed! You don't know that there are such things as grown-up children, who will take their share of sweetmeats. Well, what was in the next?

3RD CH. I thought *you* had no curiosity, and would not take advantage of mine.

1ST CH. Certainly *I* wouldn't have looked; and you may keep it all to yourself, if you like.

ALL. No, no; do tell us.

3RD CH. Well, there was the most lovely collection of toys: beautiful dolls, Noah's arks, carts, and I don't know what else. Those, of course, must be intended for us.

2ND CH. No doubt; and they are ours by right. But I know that my dear mother will insist on keeping and taking care of mine for me, and only lend them to me on some grand occasion, or when she thinks I am *very* good; which I am sorry to say is not often.

SEVERAL. That is too bad, Barbara.

1ST CH. Here come our village dames.

SCENE III.—*The same*, PLUMPER, ZUCKER, SEMMEL, &c.

PLUMP. Here you are, children; always first when anything is to be got, and last when anything is to be learnt; as my man Karl, that is the Burgomaster, says every morning to little May· at school hour.

1ST CH. But, Mother Plumper, we were told to come; and Lotte taught us always to obey.

PLUMP. Lotte, Lotte, always Lotte. Haven't you forgotten her yet?

2ND CH. No, nor never will. Won't she come to the feast?

ZUCK. I should think *not*, indeed. The Countess is giving *us*, her tenants, a grand treat: she knows very well what we have thought it our duty to do by Lotte. And so you think she would feast us just after it, if she disapproved of it?

SEM. On the contrary, I should think she expressly wishes to show her concurrence in it.

CHILDREN. Poor Lotte! Poor Lotchen!

PLUMP. Silence, you naughty children. Do you imagine that the Countess, who is such a religious lady, would countenance a person, an utter stranger, who, for the first time, has brought a wicked witch upon her property?

Sem. Well, at any rate, *she* has disappeared forever, unless that foolish girl brings her back.

Zuck. But, Dame Plumper, what is the meaning of this festival? You ought to know.

Plump. Well, I think that, if any one does, I ought. Mam'selle Bertha gives me all her confidence, and my husband, as Burgomaster, has a right to know all that goes on, and of course has no secrets from me.

Sem. Then is that story true, about a great lady having come to the castle, and having to come here to-day?

Plump. Quite true. An immensely rich and noble lady is come to visit the Countess, who did not know her. But she seems to be really the heiress of all her estates; and she wants to bring her to see the village in holiday trim. I only hope she will not be very grand.

2nd Ch. Oh, I hope she will be as grand as possible.

3rd Ch. Will the Countess not bring her in her grand state carriage-and-four?

Plump. No, child; they are to walk quietly down, but they will go back through the village in state.

1st Ch. Oh, what a fine sight it will be. How I long to see this new lady, our future mistress!

ZUCK. For my part, I only hope she may prove
   half as good as the present.

SEM. Aye, half as indulgent to her tenants.

ZUCK. Or as charitable to the poor.

PLUMP. Or as gracious to the respectable inhab-
   itants.

2ND CH. Or as kind to children.

PLUMP. It will not be easy to have another like
   Countess Anna.   But it is getting late.   Ha!
   Miss Bertha; with Gretchen, too!

SCENE IV.—*The same, with* BERTHA *and* GRETCHEN.

PLUMP. Miss Bertha, when may we expect the
   Countess?

BER. In a few minutes.   She has left the castle.

1ST CH. And the great lady with her?

BER. Yes, child; and I am sure you will be glad
   to see her.

2ND CH. Why should we be?   For my part, I'm
   sure I would much rather see Lotte again.   But
   it seems she is not to come to the feast.

BER. Why not, I should like to know?

       [*Children clap their hands.*]

PLUMP. I thought, that is, we all thought, that
   after what had happened, you know,——

BER. Indeed, I don't know anything, except that

the Countess wishes every one to enjoy her feast, and certainly has not excluded Lotte.

ZUCK. Mam'selle Bertha, you know there is still a blank of a name in the chorus which we have been learning. Ought we not to know the name of the great lady in whose honor it is, that we may put it in?

BER. Of course, you will know it in due time. You will learn it in a moment when told you.

PLUMP. [*aside to Bertha.*] Mam'selle, it is really becoming late, and—and—you know it is rather disparaging, as my Karl, the Burgomaster, calls it, to keep the principal dames of the village waiting for an appointment. It lessens, you know,——

BER. They are coming—I hear the click of the latch at the gate.

[*All look that way : no one appears.* GRET. *goes among the children, on the other side.*]

GRET. Now, my dear children, they are coming. Behave yourselves well.

ALL. Never fear, Gretchen ; the Countess shall see that we know how to behave, even before persons of rank.

[*All continue looking towards the gate.*]

SEM. I fear it has been a false alarm! Nobody seems to be coming.

[Suddenly the children shriek out in alarm; the elder throw them-selves into attitudes, and exhibit gestures of dread, as LOTTE *slowly approaches, with the Witch on her arm, as before, totter-ing and shaking, till they reach the middle of the stage, where they stand, forming the centre of the group.]*

GRET. [*to the children, keeping them from running away.*] Now, dear children, don't be afraid. I heard you say in the wood that you would fear nothing that Lotte was with. See, there she is.

PLUMP. How insolent! ⎫ [*All at once, shrinking*
ZUCK. How horrible! ⎬ *aside.*]
SEM. How wicked! ⎭ ALL. The witch! the hag!

PLUMP. [*out of breath, and pressing her chest.*] Miss Lotte, are you not ashamed to appear here after all that has happened?

ZUCK. Yes, you bold girl, go away, do; it is too bad.

SEM. To make everybody else miserable, and spoil our feast. Do go.

LOTTE. You may well suppose, ladies, that I have not come here for my own enjoyment. But I was told that the lady of the feast would not come if I was excluded—I do not know why, for I have never seen her.

PLUMP. What! the new great lady?

LOTTE. Yes.

PLUMP. [*laughing contemptuously.*] Very likely, indeed.

BER. It is indeed quite true. I told Lotte of it myself.

SEM. Well, that *is* puzzling.

LOTTE. But besides that reason, I had another, which was irresistible.

ZUCK. Pray, what was that?

LOTTE. That I found this poor old lady sitting on the road-side, not being able to get here for the feast; and she asked me to give her my arm, which of course I could not refuse.

PLUMP. Of course: you could refuse nothing to your old friend, the witch.

ZUCK. Take her away at once, the hideous beldam.

SEM. Avaunt, wicked old witch!

CHILDREN. Oh, dear Lotty, take her away, do.

LOTTE. Shame, ladies, shame! My children, trust me. Whom among you all has this poor old and helpless creature wronged or harmed? Does not age claim reverence? Does not infirmity call for compassion? Has not hunger and weakness a better right to the enjoyment of a feast than youth and strength?

PLUMP. Feast, did you say? Do you mean to say that that wicked old thing was to sit down

with us at the treat?   I would as soon eat off a
dish that I had seen a black spider crawl over,
as partake of a feast at which she sat beside me.
Avaunt!

LOTTE. No, Frau Plumper, we will not interfere
with your enjoyment. My poor old protegée
and I will find some corner apart, or a bench
outside, at which we will gladly receive the
crumbs that you can spare us. But when you
greet loyally and affectionately your present and
your future mistresses, the prayers for blessings
from the two poorest, the aged cripple and the
homeless orphan, will be allowed above, to
mingle with yours, and they will not be re-
jected, as they are by you, with disdain.

PLUMP. Do you mean to say that you will keep
her here to face the Countess and her heiress?

LOTTE. Certainly, and without fear. I have
never seen her to speak to her, though I have
experienced her bounty. But if half that I have
heard of her is true, she will never drive away
the old and suffering from *her* feast.

PLUMP. That is very possible; she is so exces-
sively good. But that does not make it less the
duty of her faithful and loving vassals to defend her from imposture and from the intrusion
of improper characters, which witches certainly
are.

LOTTE. This is too bad! What right or reason have you to call my poor companion (who, I hope, does not hear you) by such disgraceful names?

ZUCK. Put an end to this. Do not let the Countess be insulted by the presence of such a person on her estate.

PLUMP. Who, I?

SEM. Yes, Dame Plumper; you, as the Burgomaster's wife, ought to command here.

PLUMP. I, indeed! I would not touch her for the best piece of broadcloth at Innspruck fair.

LOTTE. Once more, ladies, I appeal to your womanly and kindly feelings, if not to your charity. Have compassion on one so stricken with years and infirmities. The hand of our Heavenly Father is laid heavily upon her, that ours may lighten the burden. In doing so, it is that very Hand which sheds youth and strength on you, beauty and innocence on your children—that you take hold of and reverently raise from the curved shoulders of this His aged daughter. He loves to see His own affectionate trials no less affectionately relieved.

[*While she has been speaking,* BERTHA *has gone behind* ANNA, *and placed her hands on her shoulders.*]

PLUMP. That's right, Mam'selle Bertha, lead her

quietly out. You know best, and have courage to do what you know to be your good mistress' pleasure.

LOTTE. [*to Bertha.*] O Miss Bertha, do you go with them? Am I left alone? Am I mistaken in my estimate of the Countess' character?

BER. I must do my duty, Lotte.

LOTTE. [*weeping.*] Well, even so; I will not abandon my poor old charge, made dearer to me by the abandonment. I will lead her out.

[*The* COUNTESS *drops her stick. At the signal,* BERTHA *unclasps her cloak and draws off the hood and cloak. The* COUNTESS ANNA *stands erect, in the middle.* LOTTE *lets go her arm and modestly retreats back. All are seized with shame and astonishment.*]

ALL. The Countess! Countess Anna!

[*All are in confusion and disorder for some time.*]

PLUMP. Pardon, Madam.

ZUCK. *and* SEM. Forgive us, Countess. We did not know it was you, or else——

ANNA. Of course you did not, my good friends. However, my disguise has enabled me to hear the kind things you have said of me personally, though at the expense of the poor supposed witch. But I miss *one* here. Where is my faithful guide and fearless champion? [*Goes to*

Lotte, takes her hand, and brings her forward on her right.] Here is one who truly knows, and has taught me real charity. Till now she has never seen me, nor has she known to whom she has been kind. She intended all her goodness to be bestowed on the old, the powerless, the deformed, and the unamiable. Come, my child, and let me publicly acknowledge myself a debtor to you for the lessons you have taught me, as well as for the alms you have bestowed on me.

ALL. Alms! Is it possible?

ANNA. Yes, alms; nay, *gold.*

PLUMP. [*rather maliciously.*] Oh, then she was not so poor when she left us as some people pretended.

ANNA. No, for she was rich in virtue. But listen to the history of her alms. When I intruded on these children and frightened them *from* school—for which I am trying to make up to-day by drawing them *to* school—

CHILDREN. [*interrupting.*] O thanks, thanks! How good!

ANNA. My intention was to try this girl, who had inspired me with an inexplicable affection, from what I heard of her, and saw from a distance— an affection *quite* inexplicable to me till now.

6*

By the experiment, I wished to learn if she was really courageous in her charity, and worthy to be joined to my faithful Bertha in the distribution of my little alms.

ZUCK. Do not call them little, Madam.

PLUMP. No, indeed; we know them too well for that.

ANNA. Well, this child, Lotte, at once gave me proof of her intrepidity by supporting me and offering me harbor in her cottage. But I was not prepared for evidence of her lavish charity.

LOTTE. O dear Madam, say nothing about it; I now know how bold I was and how presumptuous to treat you so. But, indeed, I did not know you.

ANNA. Peace, child. I must do my duty. She took out a gold piece and slipped it modestly into my hand. It is to commemorate this orphan's gift that I have summoned and am going to treat you to-day.

SEVERAL. How so, Madam?

ANNA. Well, listen. I saw that the piece had been worn round the neck as a keepsake or medal, for it had a sacred figure on it. I at once recognized it as one worn by a brave young officer, once most dear to me, but killed while gallantly doing his duty. [*Weeps; Lotte starts.*]

He was Lotte's father. She is no longer, therefore, what you and I have believed her. She is
nobly born, and I have called you all together
to-day to recognize her before you all, as what
she is, and give her a position more worthy of
her birth. Henceforward she must be treated
as she deserves, and be suitably provided for.

LOTTE. [*overpowered.*] O Countess, generous and
truly noble, I deserve not all this goodness, and
especially all this public recognition and praise.
I am willing to labor for my bread, and try to
do good silently, rather than deprive the more
deserving of your bounty.

GRET. I am sure, if any one deserves every blessing, it is you, who have never failed to be good
to every one. Madam, let me be the first to
thank you for your generous reward of virtue.
Dear Lotchen is worthy of all your kindness
and honor.

ALL. Yes, yes! All blessing to Lotte!

PLUMP. But pardon me, Madam, if I am taking
a liberty in saying that we understood you had
a still greater purpose in assembling us.

ANNA. What is that?

PLUMP. We were told that we were to have the
honor of being presented, and of paying our
homage to a rich and noble lady, your guest and

heiress; whom, consequently, after the many years of happiness with which we pray heaven to bless you, our children may have to honor, though we can scarcely hope they will love as we do you, as lady of Rosenburg, and mistress paramount.

ANNA. You are quite right, Dame Plumper.

ZUCK. Will that noble dame be soon here?

ANNA. [*taking Lotte by the hand.*] She is already before you. This is that high-born and worthy lady, heiress by birth, as well as by deserts, of all my worldly estate, and of much more.

PLUMP. Most marvellous!
ZUCK. How wonderful!
SEM. How extraordinary!   } *All at once in great amazement.*

ANNA. A few words will explain all. But first, come to my heart, my darling niece! I have done violence to my feelings thus far, for your sake, but now I can bear it no longer. [*They embrace in tears and sobbing.*] To have seen so much virtue in one so young did indeed delight me. But to have discovered in one so close and dear to me, by holiest ties, is beyond my hopes or deserts.

I told you that to Lotte's alms—I must still call you so——

LOTTE. Oh, yes, yes, always. Never call me anything but Lotte.

THE CHILDREN. [*clapping their hands.*] Yes, Lotchen, Lotchen, nothing else.

ANNA. Well, to those alms you owe your present festival. The officer, by whom I recognized it, having been worn from boyhood, and who was Lotte's father, was my dear brother, the Count Ludwigron Rosenburg. Had not Lotte's extreme charity prompted her to part with so precious a memorial, to relieve an old witch, as everybody thought her, she might have remained a village schoolmistress all her life. The train thus begun was followed up. Lotte carried about her papers which, though incomplete, through my dear brother's death, furnished the clue to certain information that leaves no doubt that she is his child by a marriage which he had no time to make known. And her mother's death left her a helpless orphan, in a distant province. And to confirm all, better proof to my affections than all the lawyer's parchment, is this miniature left by her mother to her. [*Taking it out.*]

BER. And pardon me, Madam, if I have reserved till now a discovery which I made only this morning.

LOTTE. What is that? [*Eagerly.*]

BER. Besides the perfect likeness of her brother,

which the Countess found in the front of the locket, I discovered that the back opened with a spring, concealing locks of two persons' hair, with the names in enamel of Count Ludwig and Charlotte Bluhm.

LOTTE. [*starting and agitated.*] My dear mother's name.

GRET. Yes, and yours, ever since I have known you.

ANNA. Then there is no doubt of this : that you have in this my niece, the true heiress of my brother, real Count of Rosenburg. All that you see is her's—that castle, that village, and all the family estates. I have kept them carefully for such a chance, and shall retire to my own, my mother's property.

LOTTE. No, never, never let that be. I entreat and implore you not to leave the spot on which your virtues are adored by all your people.

PLUMP. No, indeed, you must not leave us, Countess! The young and new lady will enjoy all our confidence and affection, for we have now learnt her real worth.

ZUCK. And I am sure she will forgive any past misunderstanding.

CHILDREN. We have always loved you, Lotte ; won't you come and see us, and bring the Countess with you?

LOTTE. To be sure I will.

GRET. As for me, I can only ask to be your maid, to be with you sometimes. [*Bashful and sorrowful.*]

ANNA. Her maid? You, her truest and best friend? No, I am sure you will continue such, and be to her what my faithful Bertha is to me: my right hand and true heart in doing and advising the little good I am able to do.

LOTTE. A thousand thanks, dearest aunt; but how shall I learn the new duties of this unexpected condition of life without the wisdom of your advice and the example of your virtues? No, we must not separate.

ANNA. Then be it so. I do not think we shall quarrel.

PLUMP. [*cheerfully.*] We now know what name to put in our song. But how shall we distinguish in future between our two countesses?

ANNA. Oh, you must call Lotte iu future by the title.

SEM. And you, Madam?

ANNA. [*laughing.*] Oh, you may call me the " Witch of Rosenburg."

GRET. [*pertly.*] No, indeed, Madam. Pardon me, but as you have placed me in Lotchen's household, it is my duty to defend her rights and claim her titles.

ANNA. Well, how is she a witch? She has not appeared in a red cloak, nor with a broomstick.

GRET. No, Ma'am; but still I maintain her right to the name. She has scarcely been three months here, and she has fascinated all the children of the village, so as to make them love her dearly. Is it so, children?

CHILDREN. Yes, yes, indeed.

GRET. As for myself, I do not know what philtores or love potions she has used; but she has certainly bewitched me to fondness for her, such as I have never felt for any one else. You must answer for yourself, Countess.

ANNA. Truly, I can say the same. Go on.

GRET. She has thrown a spell over those ladies which has completely changed them towards her; for I am sure they honor and love her virtues as well as respect her rank.

PLUMP, &c. We do, we do, most heartily.

GRET. Only one thing remains which only a witch can do.

BER. What is that?

GRET. Transform herself.

ANNA. How has Lotte done this?

GRET. She has transmuted herself, not into a hare, or a black cat, or an owl; but into a Countess from a schoolmistress, and from a poor orphan girl into, Madam, your dear child.

ANNA. Bravo, Gretchen, you are right. Lotte's has been the true magic, for it has required but one *charm* to do all this.

ALL. And what is that?

ANNA. *Virtue.*

CHORUS.

I.

WOMEN.

Up, from mountain, plain and valley,
Huntsmen, peasants, rise and rally
   Round our hospitable Dame;
Peal aloud your* horns and voices
Till the dimmest peak rejoices
   In the echo of her name.

   [*This is repeated by men's voices, with hunting-horns accompaniment, very distant, like an echo of the women's song.*]

II.

WOMEN.

For this day both birth and merit

MEN.

   [*Repeat as above, but nearer.*]

   * *Our* in the men's repetition.

7

WOMEN.

Give us one who shall inherit

MEN.

[*Repeat, nearer still.*]

WOMEN.

All the virtues of her race:

MEN.

[*Repeat, nearer.*]

ALL.

[*The men close, though not seen.*]

Long live Lotchen, fearless maiden,
Be her head with blessings laden,
Radiant be her brow with grace.

The End.

EPILOGUE.

SPOKEN BY GRETCHEN.

I.

As once his walk the good St. Philip took,
　　Along the *Chiesa Nuovo's* corridor,
He met a father, with demurest look,
　　Creeping along the wall to the church door.

II.

Standing in front, he brought *him* to a stand,
　　Leaning upon his trusty walking staff;
And with his well-worn rosary in hand,
　　Eyed him so quaintly as to make him laugh.

III.

Then said : " My father, whither on so fast?"
　　" Not *very* fast," the old man said, " but soon
'Twill, after twenty-one,* strike the half-past;
　　And 'tis my turn to preach this afternoon."

V

" To preach : is that all? Please to go up-stairs,
　　And for my children a nice drama write;
Better to make them happy, than say prayers,
　　In whom good angels take their chief delight."

* The Italian hours used to run to twenty-four, which was,
all the year round, half an hour after sunset.

V.

" But, Father Philip, crowds are in the church:
  You would not rob them of this means of grace?"
"Oh, no ! we must not leave them in the lurch:
  Tell Father Chrysostom to take your place.

VI.

" He's always ready.   *Any* one can preach,
  But very few, like you, can write a play."
" And fewer can, like you, dear Philip, teach
  How, than to preach, 'tis better to obey."

VII.

Now, you those kindly spirits imitate,
  Clergy or laity, our good honored frier ,
Who come our feast to share or consecra e ;
  He highest draws our thanks, who lov est bends.*

* Addressed to the Bishop, if pre at.

𝔏. 𝔇. 𝔖.

"THE HIDDEN GEM,"

A

DRAMA IN TWO ACTS.

"THE HIDDEN GEM."

A

DRAMA IN TWO ACTS.

COMPOSED FOR THE COLLEGE JUBILEE OF

SAINT CUTHBERT'S. USHAW. 1858.

BY

H. E. CARDINAL WISEMAN,

————— —

NEW YORK:

P O'SHEA, PUBLISHER,

45 WARREN STREET.

1*

PROLOGUE

TO "THE HIDDEN GEM."

Recited at the performance of that drama by the members of the Catholic Institute of St. Philip Neri, at Liverpool, on the 26th of January, 1859.

UNSCARED by menace, unreformed by age,
Deaf to the voice of prophet, priest, and sage,
Despite Experience's instructive rules,
The pith of proverbs, and the lore of schools,
Which tell, in words of wisdom from of old,
How all that glitters is not therefore gold;
The knowing world, in changeless accents, cries,
"The gold that glitters is the gold *I* prize."
  Yet might the world its eye sagacious turn
To Nature's truthful tablets, there to learn
The ways and workings of mysterious Grace,
In type reflected on Creation's face;
Sure it had known how precious things of earth
On hearts unthankful waste their useless worth;

How gifts of goodliest form and fairest bloom
Lurk in the deep, or slumber in the gloom;
How caves unfathomed hide the priceless ore,
And pearls of ocean strew the desert shore,
And sweetest flowers of summer live and die,
Unseen, unheeded, save by Angel's eye:
Taught by these monitors, the world might know
How purest treasure oft may poorest show.

O, knew we but our bliss, the happiest we,
To whom 'tis given this gracious truth to see,
Not couched in emblem, nor by hint conveyed,
But in the Church's book to Faith displayed!
For sure the Church is that prolific Field,
Whose depths unsearched no answering produce
    yield;
She is that Garden, where the gifts of Spring
On arid winds their fruitless fragrance fling;
The Casket she, where gems unnoticed lie,
The staple of Heaven's beauteous jewelry.

A gem like this, so hidden, yet so bright,
We set before you, Christian friends, to-night.
The young Alexius, rich and nobly born,
Gave all to God; then, "lonely, not forlorn,"
By men despised, but full of heavenly joy,
He roamed from place to place, a pilgrim boy;
Then, sped by holy warnings back to Rome,
He lived a stranger in his childhood's home;

And, worthiest he the son's award to share,
Chose the slave's part, and prized the menial's
    fare;
Till, in Affliction's furnace tried and proved,
Spurned where he trusted, slighted where he
    loved,
He laid him down and died. But Truth hath
    said,
" The corn of wheat first liveth, when 'tis dead ; "*
So he, I ween, did pass through bitter strife,
From living death to bright undying life.
    Saint Philip's children, in Saint Philip's name,
Not your applause, but your indulgence claim ;
Fain would they proffer, in this simple Play,
Saint Philip's truth in his own childlike way.
Yet, might your genial smile once beam on them,
This Tale itself might prove "a hidden gem,"
In flowers illusive wrapt. For not alone
The moor's drear vastness, or the desert's stone,
O'erlays the mine which teems with embryo
    wealth,
Or hides the fount whence issue streams of health ;
The ore may sleep beneath the garden's crest,
The blue waves laugh† around the jewel's nest,

---

* St. John, 12: 21, 25.

† ανήριθμον γέλασμα πόντου.—Æschyl.

And woods of emerald foliage lure the eye
To where deep springs of health embedded lie.*
And thou, dear Prince, in loving presence here,†
Our toil to lighten, and our hearts to cheer;
Wont from the care of Churches to descend,
At prayer of children, or at suit of friend,
If haply, like Saint Philip, thou may'st win
Some wayward soul from error, or from sin;
Thou art the pole-star of our course to-night;
If thou be near, the lowering sky grows bright;
What frown shall scare us, if we feel *thy* love?
What critic dare to blame, if *thou* approve?

F. CAN. O.

---

* It is often remarked that mineral springs are found in the midst of romantic scenery.

† The writer feels it necessary to observe, in explanation, that His Eminence, Cardinal Wiseman, was present on the occasion for which this Prologue was written.

THE ARGUMENT.

In the reign of the Emperor Honorius and the Pontificate of Innocent I., there lived on the Aventine, a Roman Patrician of great wealth, named Euphemianus. He had an only son, Alexius, whom he educated in principles of solid piety, and in the practice of unbounded charity. When he was grown up, but still young, a Divine command ordered the son to quit his father's house, and lead the life of a poor pilgrim. He accordingly repaired to Edessa, where he lived several years, while he was sought for in vain over all the world. At length he was similarly ordered to return home; and was received as a stranger into his father's house.

He remained there as many years as he had lived abroad, amidst the scorn and ill-treatment of his own domestics, until his death: when first a voice, heard through all the churches in the city, proclaimed him a Saint, and then a paper, written by himself, revealed his history.

As the years passed by Alexius in these two conditions have been variously stated by different writers, in this Drama they have been limited to five spent in each, or ten in all.

The beginning and the close of the second period, of that passed at home, form the subject of this composition; so that five years are supposed to elapse between its two acts.

Such is the domestic history recorded in Rome, on the Aventine Hill, where the beautiful church of St. Alexius yet stands, and is visited, on his feast, by crowds of his fellow-citizens. The view from its garden is one of the most charming in Rome. The basilica of Santa Sabina is next door to it.

DRAMATIS PERSONÆ.

EUPHEMIANUS, a Roman Patrician.

ALEXIUS, under the name of *Ignotus*, his son.

CARINUS, a boy, his nephew.

PROCULUS, his Freedman and Steward

EUSEBIUS, freed after Act I.

BIBULUS, ...

DAVUS, ... >Slaves.

URSULUS, } Black, . . .

VERNA, }

GANNIO, a Beggar.

AN IMPERIAL CHAMBERLAIN.

AN OFFICER.

SLAVES, white and black.

TWO ROBBERS.

SCENE on the Aventine Hill in Rome, partly outside, partly
in the court or Atrium, of Euphemian's house, in the
Reign of Honorius, and the Pontificate of Innocent I.

(13)

"THE HIDDEN GEM."

ACT I.

SCENE I.—*An open space on the Aventine, with houses on one side, and trees on the other. At the back is the door of Euphemian's house. Under the trees is a marble bench.*

Enter ALEXIUS, *tired, wearing a cloak. Sits for a moment to rest, then rises.*

ALEXIUS. Thus far I feel, that to the very letter
I have obeyed the clear commands of heaven.
" Where first thine eyes saw light, there must
    they close:
Where first thy life began, there shall it end."—
Such were the words the voice mysterious spake.
So, longing to complete my pilgrimage,
Once more I stand, where haughty Aventine
Crushes, with craggy heel, the serpent neck
Of writhing Tiber; while, between the peaks
Of Sabine hills, the sun shoots forked beams,
Hanging the gems of morning on each leaf.
  If Italy, or Rome, or Aventine

Was meant, my goal is reached—but oh, re-
    mains there
One step more, o'er that threshold—[*looking to-
    wards Euphemian's house*]—*there* to die?
For there I first drew breath.—It cannot be.
    Five years it is to-day, since I was sent,
Like him of Ur, from father's house and kin-
    dred.
What sorrow, perhaps worse, hath been endured
For me, within the compass of those walls!
Livest thou yet, sweet mother? Dost thou
    shake
Thy palsied head and quivering hand, in an-
    guish,
O'er thy long-lost, but unforgotten child?
Or dost thou, from thy patiently won throne,
Look down and smile, upon thy pilgrim son?—
I know my father lives; his name is written
Upon the dypticks of far-distant churches,
As on men's hearts, in charity's gold letters.—
How can I stand before him? How address
    him?
How if perchance he knows me?—Fathers' eyes
Are keen at spying prodigals afar,
Through fluttering tatters, and begriming dust.
    Prodigal! What a name! Have I been such?
True I was young, and rosy-cheeked, and rich.

The night I left; but oh! 'twas not to plunge
Into the golden bath of luxury,
Or play the spendthrift. Bitter tears rolled
    down,
As sobs heaved panting from my breaking heart.
His word, who, on the Galilean sea,
Reft John from Zebedee, and changed his love,
Alone could have sustained me in that hour.
'Twas He who said: "Leave *them* and follow
    Me!"
    But see—the door is opening—who comes
    forth?
'Tis he! my father! Heaven give me strength!
                     [*Stands aside.*

Enter EUPHEMIANUS, *who sees* ALEXIUS.

EUPH. Come! a good omen, on this mournful day,
The saddest anniversary of my house.
Alms and a poor man's prayer will bless its
    grief.
Yet, though he looks both travel-sore and needy,
He asks no alms: I must accost him then.
                    [*To Alexius.*
    Good youth, you seem to be in want and pain;
Can I relieve you?
ALEX.   Gladly I receive
What maketh rich and poor each other's debtors.

  2*

EUPH. [*takes out his purse, but stops.*]   Nay stay,
      it is not gold you so much want,
  As food and rest.   No place of entertainment
  Is to be found near this.   Within my house
  You shall partake of both.—Ho! there within!
ALEX. [*staying him.*] Pray, good Sir, no!
EUPH.   Friend,
      would you rob me thus
  Of my first draught of charity's sweet air,
  Which, breathed at morn, adds fragrance to our
      prayer?
ALEX. That balmy oblation you have offered up;
  For your first words spoke charity.   A crust
  Softened in yonder fountain, and for bed
  This marble seat, will give me food and rest.
EUPH. Nay, friend, it shall not be.   I have not
      learnt
  My gospel so, that a poor man shall lie
  At my gate, wanting crumbs, sore, clad in rags,
  While I, in purple raiment, feast within.
ALEX. But, Sir, I am a palmer, used to sleep
  On the bare ground,—
EUPH.   So much the more I wish
  To have you in my house for a few hours.
  Since you, no doubt, have visited abroad
  Shrines, sanctuaries, and venerable places:
  And have stored up some holy histories,
  Which I should love to hear.—

ALEX.   Some such I know,
  And later will wait on you, to relate.
EUPH. No, friend, it shall be now.   While I but
    go,
  For holy rites, to Blest Sabina's church,
  Next to my house, do you go in, and rest.
ALEX. [*aside.*] Thank heaven! he hath not dis-
    covered me.
EUPH. [*goes to the house door.*] Come forth here.
    some one!

Enter PROCULUS.

PROC.   I am at your bidding.
      [*Looks suspiciously and contemptuously at Alexius.*]
EUPH. Good Proculus, take in this holy pilgrim,
  And give him of the best.
PROC. [*coldly.*]   It shall be done.
                           [*To Alexius.*
  Comest thou from afar?
ALEX.   Last night I landed
  At Ostia's quay, from Syria's sacred coast,
  And, in the cool of night, gained Rome and
    Aventine.
EUPH. Then truly you need rest: Proculus,
    hasten,
  And let a chamber quickly be prepared.
PROC. It is impossible!   And for a stranger—

One utterly unknown ! [*To Alexius.*] Was there
    not plague in Syria,
When thou didst there embark ?

ALEX.   None that I heard of.
    But I'm aware I am myself a plague,
    In such vile rags, unfit for dainty chambers.
    Let me repose beneath these shady trees.

PROC. [*drawing Euph. aside, while Alex. retires.*]
    Sir, as an old, I trust a faithful servant,
    Let me speak freely. It is rash and dangerous
    Thus to give lodging, even for one hour,
    To such a thing as that. There may be a plot
    To rob or murder ;—there may harbor in him
    Deep-lurking maladies,—nay foul contagion
    From Asia's swamps, or Afric's tainted coast.

EUPH. And yet the day will come, when One
    shall say,
    " I was a stranger, and you took me in,"—
    Yes, One who lurks in the outcast and the beg-
    gar
    Will speak thus to the rich.

PROC.   Then not to you.
    Doomsday will find you poor. Your lavish alms
    Would eat up your estates, were they twice
    doubled.
    Forgive plain speaking. Through the day and
    night

This is my anxious thought!

EUPH.   Nay, call it godless!
For blessed charity is not a canker,
Which gnaws, like vice, into our paltry wealth:
Charity is not rust, nor moth, nor robber.
But holy alms are like the dew of heaven,
A moisture stolen from the field by day,
Repaid with silent usury at night.

PROC. [*peevishly.*] Then be it so. I will procure
    him food.

EUPH. And place of rest.

PROC.   Where, Sir?

EUPH.   No matter where,
So that it be where charity suggests.

PROC. We have no chamber vacant, but—

EUPH.   Go on.

PROC. The one which this day five years was left
    empty.

EUPH. Rather mine own than that. None shall
    lie in it,
Till poor Alexius rest him there again.

ALEX. [*starting.*] Once more I pray you—

EUPH.   Not another word,
But follow Proculus within. I fear
I've been, through too much courtesy, uncourte-
    ous.
What is your name, good friend?

ALEX.   *Ignotus*, Sir.

I pray you, let me bear you company
To the fair temple of Sabina.   There
Would I fain sanctify this day, to me
Most blessed at its dawn, now doubly blest
In my thus meeting you.

EUPH.   I bid you welcome.

                              [*Exeunt together.*

PROC. Smooth, canting hypocrite!—but I will foil
     thee!

Twine round his soft old heart—thence will I
     pluck thee!

Come with him to his house—out I will drive
     thee!

No, not six hours shall this new friendship last,

The "Unknown" shall be thy *future* name, if
     not thy past.   [*Exit.*

SCENE II.—*The Atrium of Euphemianus's house.   The street
door at the right of the stage: the entrance to the interior of the
house on the left.   In the middle, at the back of the stage, a
small room with closed door, under a staircase.   A table in the
middle covered with a cloth reaching to the ground; behind it an
arm-chair.*

Enter BIBULUS *from the house side, cautiously looking round;
then he turns towards the door.*

BIB. It's all right, all right, come in.   The coast
is clear, and will be, for at least a good hour.

Enter URSULUS, *and all the other slaves, while and black, first timidly, bearing various utensils of household, garden, and stable work, ladles, brushes, rakes, curry-combs, &c. They range themselves on either side,* BIBULUS *going behind the table. After the others,* EUSEBIUS *enters quietly, holding a book, and stands in the background.*

URS. What have we been all brought together for?

BIB. You shall hear presently.

DAV. Stay a moment: for there is no *Nostrum** prepared, for you to *dress* us from. So I will make one. [*Turns the chair round and Bibulus mounts it.*] Thus I make one out this *crural†* chair, that is to say, an *arm-chair*, you see.

BIB. Now, comrades, I am come to speak to you about our manifold wrongs. I have been shamefully treated. Of course, when I say shamefully, I mean shamelessly.

SEVERAL. How so?

BIB. How so? Why I have been shut up all night in a dungeon—in a cellar—a dry cellar, mind, together with empty barrels, carcasses from which the spirits had long departed; and I have been bitten all night by mosquitoes. And all for nothing!

ALL. Shame! shame!

---

* Rostrum   † Curule.

Bib. Will you stand this? Will you allow your rights to be thus trampled on?

Dav. Rights? Why you said you came to speechify to us about our wrongs; and now you talk about our rights. Which is it?

Bib. Booby! Do you not know that the more wrongs a man has, the more rights he has? He must have all his wrongs set to rights.

Verna. To be sure, Bibulus makes it quite plain. All wrongs are all rights. Aren't they?

Bib. Exactly.

Dav. And therefore *wiser worser*, all right is all wrong.

Bib. That's it. That's your modern *plitical economy*.

Ver. So right or wrong, it's all one. Hurrah!

All. Hurrah! hurrah!

Bib. So it was right you see,—no, it was wrong— let me see, well it was either right or wrong, as the case may be, to keep me in prison all night; and so your rights were wronged in me.

Urs. But you haven't told us what it was for.

Dav. Aye, tell us *our* rights that *you* were wronged for.

All. Yes, yes! what was it for?

Bib. Why for a paltry flask or two of wine, which I drank to master's health.

VER. Then if I understand the matter, we were wronged in not having our share of it. That was *our* right; and it was *you* who wronged us! Down with him!

ALL. Aye, down with him! [*They rush towards him.*]

EUSEB. [*laughing, steps forward to check them.*] Come, friends, enough of this folly. The long and short of the matter is, that he walked into his master's *hock,* and so the master walked him into his *quod.* That's a perfect concord, agreeing in gender, number, and case; and therefore if one agreed with *him* the other did too.

BIB. I think it's the wrong case altogether; for certainly *hock* agrees with me, and *quod* doesn't! But let us have common sense, and none of this cram!

DAV. Yes, yes, Bibulus is right—common sense, now! Let us by all means have common sense.

EUSEB. Very well. Let me ask, is not the wine the master's property?

SEVERAL. Of course it is.

EUSEB. He has a right to keep it in an amphora in his cellar.

BIB. Aye, till we can get at it.

EUSEB. Hold your tongue till I have done. And

3

if it be poured, as usual, into a sheepskin, may he not still lock it up in his inner cellar?

SEV. Certainly, what then?

EUSEB. Or if into an ass's skin, does that make any difference?

SEV. Of course not.

EUSEB. Then that is just the case.

ALL. How?

EUSEB. Pray what is the difference between its getting into Bibulus's skin, and into any *other* donkey's skin? Had not the master an equal right to lock it up in his cellar? And that's just what he did.

ALL. Bravo, bravo! Bibulus is an ass.

BIB. [*furious.*] I'll pay you out for this, one day, Eusebius. Listen, my friends. All this comes of bad logic, as one may say: of putting the premises before the consequence. I'll teach you right logic. Pray what was wine made for?

URS. To be drunk, of course.

BIB. Well, then, let that wiseacre tell you how wine is *to be* drunk, without *being* drunk.

VER. Very good.

BIB. Then you see, in being drunk, I only did what wine was made for: *ergo,* I did quite right.

DAV. And therefore quite wrong.

BIB. But the fact is, the wine is as much mine as Euphemian's. Who gave *him* the soil? Who gave *him* the vines? Nature made them both, and nature gives them as much to me as to him. Before nature we are all equal.

ALL. To be sure we are!

BIB. Then why is not the wine mine as much as Euphemian's?

EUSEB. Because you did not make it.

BIB. Neither did he.

ALL. True, quite true!

BIB. One man has no right to the produce of many others' labor! If we are all equal, it is clear that all things should be in common! Down with artificial distinctions, say I. Why should one man wear broad-cloth, and another long-cloth? One drink Falernian, and another Sabine? Tell me that!

EUSEB. Come, Bibulus, you are getting venomous. Let us be equal. Why should you stand on a chair, and we on the ground? You have all the talk, and we only listen!

SEV. Go on! go on!

VER. [*shaking a rake.*] I like this wholesale way of levelling; it beats rake husbandry hollow. But how could we make a right division? Lay all out in flower-beds, as one may say.

Bib. Oh, very easily. You should have the garden : Eusebius might take the library, and welcome.

Euseb. Thank you, and how live?

Bib. Why, haven't I heard you say that you *devour* new publications, *relish* a good poem, and would like to *digest* a code of laws? Haven't you often declared, that in a certain book there was want of *taste*, that another was a *hotch-potch*—that one writer was *peppery*, and another *spicy*, a third *insipid*, or that, poor wretch! he had been terribly *cut up*, or made *mince-meat* of, and completely *dished*, by those cannibals called critics?

Dav. Bravo, Bibulus; you have settled *his* hash, at any rate. Now for the rest.

Bib. Well, then, Strigil might have the stables and horses, Fumatus the kitchen, and I—the cellar.

Sev. No, no; that must be common property.

Urs. This is all very fine: but how are we to get at our own? Would Euphemian do it kind, and give up?

Bib. [*hesitating and deliberating.*] Well, on that point, I do not clearly see my way. Belling the cat, eh? I can't see, unless we set the house on fire—

URS. Nay, that would be destroying all our property.

BIB. [*aside.*] Except the cellar. [*Aloud.*] Still, that would be a noble way of asserting our rights.

DAV. To be sure it would, and it would be great fun!

EUSEB. Come, Bibulus, enough of this fooling. You are now becoming mischievous, and treacherous too. My friends and comrades, you cannot be so mad as to dream of such wickedness and absurdity.

URS. [*doggedly.*] Well, then, at least let us have the satisfaction of setting some one else's house on fire. It will be some compensation for being trampled under foot at home.

SEV. Whose shall it be?

BIB. I like the idea, as a sort of distraction, you know, from our own grievances. Let me see. Oh yes! there are plenty of neighbors not far off. Their people seem tolerably comfortable, and their houses are in good order. But there are some in them that would like to see a good flare up; and why have not we a right to give it them?

EUSEB. Why so?

BIB. Why so? Why for fifty reasons. First, they

3*

don't eat beef as we do. They *ought* to eat beef.

VER. So they ought. That's a capital reason; what else?

BIB. Then they are not like us. Not one of them dare talk openly of setting his master's house on fire, as I do. We are free.

UUSEB. And easy.

DAV. Aye, free and easy. That's the age, Sir. We don't care for *Harry's toggery:* we are all for *demonocracy.* Aren't we?

ALL. To be sure we are.

BIB. We don't mind masters or stewards.—Do we?

ALL. Not we.

BIB. We'll pitch them all out of the window.— Won't we?

ALL. That we will.

BIB. Beginning with Proc—Hallo! There he comes.

[*Leaps down and dives under the table*]

Enter PROCULUS. *All look sheepish.*

PROC. Well, gentlemen, what is the meaning of this strange meeting in the hall? How come you to be all here, instead of minding your work? Come, speak, some of you. I heard noise enough just now.

DAV. Why, Sir, do you see, as this is the sorrowful hanniversary of the family, we thought it shootable to hold a sort of conwiwial meeting, just to poke up its affliction. So we have been talking over our wrongs.

PROC. Your *wrongs?*

VER. That is, our *rights*, you know, Sir.

PROC. Better still. This must be some of Bibulus's work. I am sure I heard his voice—where is he?

DAV. He has absquatulated, Sir; but I think he can hardly have got a mile off yet.

PROC. He shall be caught in due time, and shall get his deserts. [Bibulus *peeps from under the table, and shakes his fist at* Proculus, *who does not see him. All laugh.*] What are you all laughing at? He will find it no laughing matter, I can tell you. However, as you *are* here, I may as well give you a piece of news.

ALL. What is it?

PROC. Why, that your master has just now taken a fancy to a beggar.

ALL. A beggar?

PROC. Aye, a beggar, a man calling himself a pilgrim, whom he wishes to bring into the house, to sleep here, and to eat and drink of the best. So he commands. And consequently to be *dutifully* waited on by you.

Urs. That's a downright shame!

Dav. We won't stand it! It's quite beneath us.

Ver. We won't sit down under it! We're quite above it.

Proc. [*ironically.*] Oh, but, no doubt, you will do all in your power to make him comfortable.

Dav. Oh, to be sure!

Proc. When he is asleep, you will take care to make no noise near, to disturb him.

Ver. Of course we will.

Proc. And if your master sends dainties to him, you will not intercept them, but will see that he is well fed, and gets sleek and fat.

Urs. Won't we!

Proc. He will have an easy life of it,—won't he, now?

All. Trust us for that! A beggar, indeed!

Proc. Well, you seem pretty unanimous in that, I think.

Dav. *Quite* magnanimous, as you say, Sir. But where will he lodge, that we may know how to keep quiet?

Proc. [*pointing to the cell,*] There, under the stairs.

All. Ha! ha! ha!

Dav. He will hardly have a glimpse of light.

Ver. Or a mouthful of air.

Urs. Or room to turn round.

PROC. So he will turn *out* all the quicker.

EUSEB. [*aside.*] Why, he is as bad as Bibulus! [*To Proc.*] Sir, does our master intend his new friend to be so treated?

PROC. Hold your tongue, slave. You are always prating when you are not wanted. My men, you are all agreed?

ALL. All.

PROC. How he is to sleep?

ALL. Yes, Sir.

PROC. And to eat?

ALL. Yes, Sir.

PROC. And to be got out?

ALL. Yes, Sir.

CHORUS OF SLAVES.

I.

There shall be no rest for his aching bones,
  None to his weary head:
For his bed shall be like the torrent's stones,
  His pillow be as lead.

II.

To him shall his food no nourishment yield,
  Refreshment none his cup:
He shall eat the refuse of garth and field,
  The fetid pool shall sup.   [*Exeunt omnes.*

SCENE III.—*The same.*

Enter BIBULUS *from under the table.*

BIB. Well! I do think that I am all the better for a little sobering under the table. Really, if I had not given way from a boy to this rascally propensity of mine, I might have been the most popular leader in the Empire! See how, but for that stupid Eusebius, who always spoils everything good, I should have induced those fools of comrades to set the house on fire, and I should have obtained my revenge, and escaped in the confusion. Many a fellow has reached the Roman purple from a less promising beginning.

But as this has failed, let me set earnestly about some other plan. Again and again, I have been vilely used, down to last night. Aye, last night! That was the last drop! That can never be blotted out except by one means.—Yes, in the intense solitude of that foul dungeon,— in the Tartarus of that broiling furnace—in the murkiness of that endless night—still more, in the bitterness of an envenomed soul—in the recklessness of despair—yea, through gnashing teeth and parched throat—I, Bibulus, vowed revenge—fatal revenge. My manacles and gyves rung like cymbals, as my limbs quivered while I uttered the burning words; and a hollow moan, or laugh—I know not which—re-echoed them through the vault.

And when did an Asiatic heart retract such a vow? When did it forego the sweet, delicious thought—the only luxury of a slave—revenge?

Euphemianus, thou shalt not be long my master. Yet Euphemianus is a good master—a kind and gentle—Is it so? Then why does he allow me to be lashed every day like a hound—chained up like a ban-dog?

But it is Proculus that doth all this to thee, Bibulus.—And who is Proculus, and what is Proculus? Only the other's arm—his hand—his limb. I strike not at these—I aim straight at the brain—the heart—the soul. I do not maim or cripple—I slay, I kill.

Then, if Proculus die, what better am I? There are fifty worse than he, and ready to take his place.—Here, for example, comes one of them—

Enter EUSEBIUS.

EUSEB. Well found, Bibulus; here is something for you. [*Gives him a paper.*]

Bib. What is this? You know I am no scholar. [*Trying to read it.*]

Euseb. Why, in two words, it is an order from Proculus, who has learnt your late proceedings, telling you that you are degraded from the condition of a house servant to that of a country slave, and commanding you to proceed this very afternoon to Ardea, there to begin your labors.

Bib. [*starting.*] To Ardea! In the very heat of summer! To the most pestilential spot in the Roman territory, where the most sturdy perish in a year, unless born there! Thither am *I* to go—degraded, too!—to die perhaps in a month, like a frog on a mud-bank, when the sun has dried up its brackish pool! Has Proculus thought of this?

Euseb. Most certainly; for not only does he know it, but he observed expressly that this was a more lenient punishment than being scourged to death, as you had deserved. You would soon die out, he said, and we should be well rid of a pestilent fellow.

Bib. Better be scourged to death with scorpions than sucked to death by poisonous insects, or by a wasting miasma. Does Euphemian know of it?

EUSEB. Not yet, but no doubt he will confirm the
award.   Farewell, Bibulus; bear with courage
what you have heartily deserved. [*Exit.*]

BIB. Farewell, sycophant! farewell, indeed?   No,
not yet.—There shall be moaning over death in
this house before *I* go to encounter it.   After
this cruel doom, who will blame me if I seek
to escape it?—Yet here again comes the ques-
tion—who is doing this?   Proculus.   Then
ought not my vengeance to fall on *him?*
Warily, calmly—let us weigh this.

If Proculus dies, Eusebius would be worse.
Now, if Euphemian dies, it is very different.
We know that by his will he has released all
his slaves.   So let *him* die, and I am free.

But is this generous or honorable?   Tut,
tut; who has ever been generous or honorable
with me?   And am I to begin the virtues first?
Out upon it—no!

Yet the thing must be done cautiously, se-
curely.   It is an ugly thing, is killing, even in
revenge.   One must throw a veil over it—make
it appear like an accident, even to one's self.
Ha! happy combination—I know how at once
to procure the necessary means, and then—the
pilgrim who is going to sleep *there* [*pointing to
the cell*]—Capital! What more likely?—He

4

has some design, no doubt—and he will be the only person near. A train can be easily laid to bring it home to him.—Bravo, Bibulus, thou art a clever hand at mischief. By one blow thou shalt gain liberty, security, and—revenge! Eh?

Revenge on foes is sweet: 'tis sweeter still,
When yours is all the gain, theirs all the ill.

[*Exit.*

SCENE IV.—*The Aventine.*

Enter GANNIO, *in rags, with a wallet, affecting to be lame.*

GAN. Well, that was a wise old poet, Ennius, I think they call him, who wrote those verses:
"Of all the trades in Italy, the beggar's is the
    best,
Because, if he is tired, he can sit him down and
    rest."
So as I drive a thriving trade by begging, I will use my privilege. [*Sits down, wiping his forehead.*] I have walked twenty miles to get here, for this blessed day, the *doleful* day of the house, so called, I presume, from the liberal alms always doled out on it.

Enter BIBULUS, *unobserved.*

I am well repaid, however, for my diligence

and speed, for I am first and earliest in the field. It is clear that none of the fraternity have slipped in between me and the first pickings.

BIB. [*coming forward.*] You are wrong there, old fellow.

GAN. Good morning, Bib.; what do you mean?

BIB. Why, that a more knowing one than you has stepped in before you, and regularly done you: a young beggar, which you are not—a handsome beggar, which you never were—and a virtuous beggar, which you never will be. He was here when the master first left the house, wormed himself into his favor in no time, and is invited to eat, drink and sleep in the house—actually in the house. Orders are that he must have the best of everything. So you are cut out, at any rate!

GAN. [*enraged.*] The villain! all my precedence taken from me; my very birthright. Every praise you have uttered of him is a sting, a dagger to me. Where is he?

BIB. There he comes, with the master. [*Stands aside, while Euphemian and Alexius pass them, conversing, and go into the house.*]

GAN. Aye, there he goes! a sleek, smooth, treacherous rival!

BIB. Rival?　Why, don't you see how completely
he is at home with the master?

GAN. That I do.

BIB. You are fairly supplanted *there*, at least.

GAN. I see it.　How I should like to—[*makes a
gesture of stabbing.*]

BIB. Hush! we all dislike him as much as you.

GAN. I am glad to hear that.　But, how can it be
managed?

BIB. Gannio, you sell—you know what, eh?

GAN. Powders, to kill rats?　[*Bibulus nods.*]
Oh, yes, I always have them ready.

BIB. Are they sure in their action, and safe?

GAN. Quite.

BIB. How are they administered?

GAN. You put a pinch of the stuff into a goblet
—I mean where the rats drink; and any one—
that is, any rat—that tastes, dies, without remedy, in an instant.　No tales to tell—that is,
there is hardly time to squeak, you understand;
I speak of rats, you know.

BIB. Of course.　We should be glad to get rid
of—

GAN. A rat, mind you.　Recollect, I said so, expressly.　I have nothing to do with anything
else.　[*Draws a box out of his wallet.*]　What
will you take it in?

BIB. [*after feeling in his pocket, takes out the paper given him by Eusebius.*] Here, this will do. Is this enough?

GAN. [*putting some powder into the paper.*] Enough for a hundred and fifty of them.

BIB. And I suppose for *one* beggar.

GAN. I know nothing about *that*. But I hope I shall never hear of *him* again.   [*Exit.*

BIB. You old dotard! Do you think I am going to risk my throat to get rid of *your* enemies? I have a loftier aim. The fate of Rome's noblest patrician is folded in this little paper. But I have no time to lose.   [*Exit.*

SCENE V.—*The Atrium. A table rather on one side, so as to leave the door under the stairs free.*

Enter EUPHEMIANUS *and* ALEXIUS, *conversing.*

EUPH. Have you, perchance, Ignotus, ever met,
   Or in your travels heard of, a fair youth,
   By name Alexius?

ALEX.   No uncommon one—
   Hath he no token whereby to distinguish him?

EUPH. None, except that of a sad history—
   He was the son of an illustrious house,
   Daintily bred, and heir of boundless wealth:
   Yet as an angel, gentle, sweet, and pure.

   4*

By all beloved—by one too highly prized;
So heaven took him from him.

ALEX.   Did he die, then?

EUPH. Alas! far worse than that; he fled from
   home,
Leaving his parents desolate and crushed.
His mother melted soon away in tears,
And murmured, as she patient died, his name.
      [*Weeps.*]
This day completes his father's five years' woe.
[*Looking hard at Alexius.*] Methinks he must
   be now about your age.
Perhaps a little taller—no, the same.   [*Alexius
   tries to turn away.   Euph. holds him and
   looks in his face.*
Your eyes remind me, too, so much of his,
So blue and mild, like doves',—but he was fair,
As Phrygian marble, veined with purple blood.
Yet travel may have browned his cheek like
   yours.
His graceful mouth—yours is, no doubt, such too,
But that your beard conceals it—had a trick
So sweet, so winning, that by it alone
I could discern him from ten thousand—Ah!
You weep, good pilgrim, too: thanks for those
   tears!
Oh tell me, then, did you e'er hear of him?

ALEX. [*confused.*] Ah! yes, dear father!—I had almost said,
  You look so kind—Yes, venerable Sir—
  I do remember somewhat—let me see—
EUPH. Speak! say, for heaven's sake, what you remember.
ALEX. [*sadly.*] It is not much, I fear.
EUPH.   Still, let me hear it.
ALEX. I recollect how to Edessa came,
  Some four or five years past, well-furnished servants
  Of a great Roman lord, in quest of him;
  For I, with many, did receive their alms.
EUPH. [*sighing.*] And is this all? Alas! they found him not,
  And soon returned, to whet his parents' grief.
  Yet do I hope against all hope. His place
  Is daily kept unfilled at every meal,
  His chamber, swept and garnished, nightly waits him,
  Whom, day or night, a love unchanged will greet.
ALEX. True, faithful love is this! Yes, good Euphemian,
  Hope still, and hope: your boy will yet return.
EUPH. Ah! think you so? Or say it but to flatter
  A father's longing?

ALEX.   'Twould but ill become me
Thus to requite your love.

EUPH.   *My* love? What love?

ALEX. That hospitable love, which oft before
Hath harbored angels, why not then a son?

EUPH. Thank you, Ignotus, may your words
prove true.
I fain would learn from you your parents' names,
Where you were born, where you have spent
your youth.

ALEX. [*aside.*] Heaven protect me!

EUPH.   Well, another time,
For now, 'tis indiscretion on my part
To keep you from your needed rest—Here comes
Who shall conduct you to it. Heaven guard
you.   [*Exit.*

ALEX. And be it blest, this trial now is over,
All else seems light.

Enter PROCULUS, *who sets down refreshment.*

PROC. Sir Palmer, I fear you must be weary.
Your chamber is prepared, though it is not such
as I could have wished.

ALEX. Any hole or corner is good enough for me.

PROC. Well, I knew you would say so, wherefore
I took you beforehand at your word. You see,
though the house is large, its inmates are many.

ALEX. No doubt, plead no more, I pray.

PROC. One suite of apartments is never allowed
to be occupied; then friends often drop unex-
pectedly upon us, with large retinues—great
people, rich people, you understand? *respectable*
people.

ALEX. I beg you to spare all excuses. Anywhere
will do.

PROC. As I suppose you will only want a few
hours' rest, and then will resume your pilgrimage, a small chamber, and not very luxurious
couch, will suffice.

ALEX. Any place, good Sir.

PROC. [*showing him the cell.*] Then would it please
you to rest here?

ALEX. [*smiling.*] Most certainly—it is quite a
palace for *me*.

PROC. There is some refection for you: and may
your slumbers be refreshing. [*Exit.*

ALEX. Is this to be the sealing sleep of life,
Gluing my eyelids in unwaking rest?
Shall my heart, ere 'tis over, cease to beat,
And shall my soul awake to heaven this day?
It would appear so; for I now have reached
My place of birth, to hold it some few hours.
Here, then, must sound my last—I am prepared.
My lot is now in better hands than mine.

" Live we, or die we, we are still the Lord's."—
One prayer may serve for slumber or for death.
  Our life is Thine, Creator of all flesh,
Living or dying, wakeful or asleep.
The Hand which plays among the chords of
    life,
Pressing them gently, their vibration stills
To silence, till It wake them once again.
That Hand I kiss this day; for It hath strained
The strings of love and pain to utmost tension,
And now will soothe them with Its kindly
    touch,
To murmur peace, on Its paternal palm.
                          [Kneels.
  Father! who here this thing of clay didst
    fashion
Into Thine Image's terrestrial frame,
Its dust together hold, or free disperse,
Where rest my fathers, or are outcasts flung;
Make it the earthworm's, or the vulture's feast,
So that from its corruption flash my soul,
Into the furnace of Thy purest fire:
Or rather, like a pearl, be gently dropped
Into the abyss of Thy great ocean-bosom,
To seek in vain for surface, depth, or margin,
Absorbed, yet unconsumed, entranced, yet free.
      [Exit into his cell, closing the door.

SCENE VI.—*The same.*

Enter BIBULUS, *bearing a salver, with u goblet and food, which he lays on the table. In his right hand he holds an ewer, or flagon.*

BIB. In a few minutes, Euphemianus will come for his daily morning refection, and will find it in its usual place. He will drink it, taste it more savory, and higher spiced than usual—and will expire! What an easy and comfortable death!

[*Striking his breast.*] Down, ye growling curs of remorse! Hush! hissing worm of conscience! You are too late—the potion is mixed, and the fatal drug cannot be extracted. And then, remember Ardea—this afternoon—with its death of a mad hound foaming at the mouth, or a viper shrivelled up on a scorching bank. No; no more qualms. What I am going to do is a safe remedy of all my ills—the easiest way of gaining all my ends. And that sums up all the morality I have learnt, in these days of canting virtue!

Now let us look to our pilgrim. [*Takes out a paper, and looks into the door.*] Fast asleep; sleeps like a dead man! [*Goes in and returns.*] I never saw any one so soundly asleep. The paper is quite safe by his bedside. [*Pours out into the goblet.*] I can say the drink was nere some time; and I cannot be further responsible.—But, here comes the master—O heavens! I wish it were well over! I will stand by, and the first to give the alarm! [*Retires.*]

SCENE VII.—*The same.*

Enter EUPHEMIAN *from the street door.*

EUPH. I own I like my guest. His words are sweet;
His looks call up some image I have loved.
Then his affection seemeth almost filial,
Tender and melting at a father's woe.
I feel athirst! [*Takes the cup and is putting it to his lips, when a solemn voice procceds from the cell, the door of which has been left ajar.*]

ALEX.   EUPHEMIAN, BEWARE!
EUPH. [*starting and putting down the cup.*] Was that some play of fancy mocking me?
[*Looking about.*] No one is nigh, 'twas plainly imagination.
I have felt tempted e'en to press my guest,
As they of Emmaus theirs, to rest with me—
Perhaps declare him my adopted son!—

My lips are parched! [*Again raises the cup, and the same voice is heard.*]

ALEX. BEWARE, EUPHEMIAN!

EUPH. [*puts down the cup.*] Beware of what?
Not of this harmless draught?
Oh no; I know that voice!—'Tis dear Alexius,
Far off in body—ah! perhaps in heaven—
Who thus reproaches me for my unfaithfulness,
In putting of this pilgrim in his place.

[*Passionately.*]

It shall not be, dear son! But oh! why speak,
And not be seen? Yet still, if thou canst hear,
My child, this cup of grace I quaff to thee!

[*Waving the cup over his head. As he is just going to drink, Alexius rushes out, and dashes it from his hand*]

ALEX. Hold! It is deadly poison.

EUPH. [*loud.*] Ho! in here!

Enter PROCULUS *and slaves.* ALEX. *snatches the ewer from* BIBULUS, *and puts it on the table.* ALEX. *in the middle,* EUPH. *on his right,* PROC. *and* BIB. *on his left: the rest on either side, forward.*

PROC. What is the matter? What has happened,
Sir?

EUPH. Foul treachery and murder have been
here.
My cup was poisoned.

5

Proc.   Who hath told you so?

Alex. I.

Proc.   How do *you* know?

Dav.   Every drop is spilt.

Proc. Bibulus, you prepared it; speak! or, sirrah,
  Your life must answer.

Bib.   Sir, the cup was pure
  As heaven's dew, when here I left it. What
  May, in my absence, have befallen, I know not.
  They who have tampered with it, best can tell.

Proc. Whom do you mean? Speak plain, man,
  out at once.

Bib. Him who discovered it—how knew he of it?
  Poison there is, but in his tongue who sought
  Your heart to envenom. Put him to his proof.

Proc. Sir, Bibulus is right for once.

Euph.   There seems
  Some lack of proof indeed.

Alex.   Then here receive it.
     [*Draws out a paper.*]
  This paper in my room I found—nay, saw it
  Hastily dropped there, as I feigned deep slumber.
  Know you it, Proculus?

Proc.   O gracious heaven!
  It is the order but some hour ago
  Despatched by me to Bibulus.

EUSEB. [*looking at it.*] By me
Delivered to him.

EUPH. What does it contain?

URS. 'Tis ratsbane, I can see.

BIB. [*aside.*] Fool that I was! [*Aloud.*]
Assassins may be thieves.

ALEX. Then come to proof.
This ewer, Bibulus, was in your hand,
When here you entered; was it not?

ALL. We saw it.

ALEX. [*takes the empty cup left by Proc. and pours
into it.*] No one with *this* has tampered;
drink it then,
Before thy master's eye. [*Offers it to him.*]

PROC. Yes, drink it off.

BIB. Before his feet to die! Good master, spare
me! [*Kneeling.*]

EUPH. Oh, heavens! Thanks for such a mercy.

PROC. Sir,
Let punishment condign requite this crime.
Seize him, and bind him fast, for death.

ALL. Aye, aye, Sir.
[*They rush on him.*]

ALEX. [*interposing himself.*] Sir, in exchange for
your life saved, I ask,
Give him to me, or rather to your son,
On this his mournful day.

EUPH.   I can't refuse.

ALEX. And now for my reward—

EUPH.   Ask what you please.

ALEX. Your purse!

EUPH.   What! paltry gold?

ALEX.   Yes, yes, indeed,
    I never felt so covetous as now.
        [*Euph., astonished, gives him his purse.*]
    [*To Bibulus.*] Take this and flee. At Ostia's
      quay yet lies
    A vessel bound to Palestine; there seek
    Pardon, 'midst scenes of all-forgiving love.
                    [*Exit Bibulus.*

EUPH. As yet, Ignotus, all my debt remains
    Uncancelled, and must be so. For with life
    I owe to you, whatever gives life worth.
    This house, my fortune—all belongs to you.
      Be this my first request—we part no more.
    We share this roof, through what of life re-
      mains.
    Where are you lodged?

PROC. An't please you, Sir, by reason of some re-
    pairs, and, and—

EUPH. And what, pray?

ALEX. I am perfectly satisfied with my quarters,
    Sir.

PROC. Exactly, Sir, the gentleman being anxious
for quiet and devout retirement,—being a pilgrim, you see, Sir,—

EUPH. Come, come, tell me at once—where have
you harbored him?

PROC. [*confused, and pointing back.*] Why, *there,*
Sir.

EUPH. There? In that dog's hole hast thou ken-
nelled him?

Is that the pilgrim's welcome in my house?

Shame on thee, Proculus!

ALEX. Peace, good Euphemian.

If I had not lodged *there,* thou wouldst have died!

ALL. Very true.

ALEX. Now this chamber hath been blest
To you and me: I claim it therefore from you.
There will I live, and, if heaven pleases, die.

EUPH. Ignotus, I must yield to you. But say,
How did you learn my danger? Whose voice
heard I?

ALEX. That voice was mine.

EUPH. [*aside.*] It sounded like my child's.

ALEX. While in sound sleep, methought there
stood beside me
A being fair, but radiant as the morn.
His purple wings were tremulous with gold,
Like cedars in the breeze at set of sun.

5*

He struck my side and woke me. Then I heard
That slave's foul treachery. He entering in
With black design, believed me fast asleep,
And dropped his poisonous bait. I started up,
And, through the door neglectfully unclosed,
Saw all the rest.

EUPH.   A blessing came with you
Into my house.—But say, who was that spirit?
He entered too with you.—

ALEX.   I know him well.
He is the pilgrim's angel, he who wards
The hospitable threshold.—Mark my words.
    Four angels guard our gracious works of love,
Guide them below, and chronicle above.
The fainting, feeds from silver bowls the first,
With golden cup, the second slakes their thirst.
The third the naked clothes with broidered pall;
But HOSPITALITY unites them all,—
To clothe, feed, quicken, when his jewelled key
Opens, for harbor, home, or hostelry.
Him these three spirits tend, him glad surround,
    Who brighter works of mercy leaves to them;
While he, with seraph-gaze bent on the ground,
    Finds in the dust, and saves some "hidden
    gem."   [*Exeunt.*

END OF FIRST ACT.

ACT II.

*There is an interval of five years between the first and
second acts.*

SCENE I.—*The Atrium. Enter* EUPHEMIAN, CARINUS, *with*
EUSEBIUS, *in cloaks and petasi, or large hats.* EUSEBIUS
takes off their travelling attire, and goes out. CARINUS *has
the bulla round his neck.*

(*A couch, raised only at one end, in the apartment.*)

EUPH. Well, dear Carinus, are you tired?

CAR.   No, father;
  (Since I must call you so, by your command,)
  This morning's journey has been charming.
    What
  Could be more lovely than the Tiber's banks,
  Fringed with those marble villas, cool i'th'
    shade
  Of lazy pines, and scarcely-nodding cypresses?
  All was so still; except the gilded prows
  That shot along the water, bright, yet soft,
  As swarms of summer fire-flies.

EUPH.   Welcome, then,
  To your own goodly home.

CAR. [*looking round him.*]   A goodly home.
  It is, indeed, and fair! And yet not mine.

EUPH. Right: for to-morrow is the day appointed

For your adoption.   Then, indeed, more truly
All that you see will yours become; and more.
CAR. How can that be, your heir being still alive?
EUPH. Alas! all hope is now extinct!
CAR.   How so?
EUPH. I have in vain the whole world travelled
     through,
    Made proclamations, offered high rewards,
    And more than all, have trusted to the instincts
    Of filial love, wherever it might be,
    To claim its dues.
CAR.   If heaven had stronger claims,
    All this was vain.
EUPH.   Only three days and nights
    Did Mary's Son allow the quest for Him,
    By His dear parents—full ten years has mine.
CAR. O father! those three days were *twenty* years
    To Mary's heart!
EUPH. [*aside.*]   What wisdom hath this child!
    [*Aloud.*] My hopes are wearied out.   There-
        fore to-morrow,
    The anniversary of our long mourning,
    Shall mark our change to joy.   Honorius comes
    To honor my poor banquet.   At its close,
    Amidst the clang of trumpets and of cymbals,
    The Emperor himself will name you heir
    Of all your uncle's wealth.

CAR.   And if Alexius,
  Before the echo of those sounds be quelled,
  Appear amongst us?
EUPH.   No.   It cannot be.
  Conjure not up such fancies.   For five years
  I have been buoyed up by the hopeful speech
  Of a young holy pilgrim, who yet dwells
  Within these walls.   Ten years is long to hope!
CAR. But tell me, father, was Alexius all
  That I have heard described?   Gentle and
    sweet,
  Obedient, pure, to the distressed most kind,
  To saints devout, burning with higher love?
EUPH. All this, and tenfold more, if ten times
    told.
CAR. Then let me be the sharer of his virtues,
  Never usurper of his heritage.
  Alexius lives, and will claim back his own.
EUPH. How say you, child?
CAR.   You have described a saint,
  Such as dies not, but all the Church shall know
    it.
  Remember how, when Servulus, the mendicant,
  Died in the court of holy Clement's church,
  Our earthly psalmody was hushed, to hear
  The angels chaunt his passing-hymn outside.*

* St. Gregory's Dialogues, B. iv, c. 14.

EUPH. Oh! may it be so!   Then will he not care
  For worldly wealth or honor!

Enter EUSEBIUS.

EUSEB.   Pardon, Sir!
  The household are without, anxious to pay
  Homage to you and to their future lord.
EUPH. Let them come in!

Enter DAVUS, VERNA, *and other slaves, and range themselves
on either side.*

EUSEB.   Your servants, Sir, desire
  To welcome you again, after long absence,
  And pray you many years of home and joy.
  Dispel the cloud which hath so long o'erveiled
  The sunlight of the house.   Try to forget
  By learning how to hope!   May this young
      bloom [*Pointing to Car.*]
  Upon the household tree gracefully mantle
  The winter's past decay.
CAR.   No, good Eusebius,
  Say autumn's ripened fruit.   I'm but a boy,
  And cannot take the place of manly virtue.
  My friends, I thank you for your kindly wishes,
  And as you love me, grant me but this favor,—
  I wish not to be courted, flattered, fed
  With honeyed speeches. Let me hear the truth

From all, at all times, though that truth be
    blame.
ALL. Bravo! Bravo!
EUPH. Thanks, my good friends; such proofs of
    kindly feeling
Bind up a household in strong mutual love.
Haste now once more, each to prepare his part
For the glad morrow; when our Emperor
Will grace our board, and our new heir proclaim.
To-morrow's sun shall bleach our mourning
    palls,
And kindle joy in these ancestral halls.

                            [*Exeunt omnes.*

SCENE II.—*The same.*

Enter ALEXIUS *solus, faint and weak—sits down.*

ALEX. How long? O heavens! how long shall I
    drag on
This lingering life? Five years are on the eve
Of their completion, since I entered here.
Smoothly hath time flowed on, yet quickening
    ever
Its rapid course; and now methinks I am
Like one who nears a cataract. His skiff
Glides through a noiseless, foamless, liquid fur-
    row,

Which curves at last over the craggy ledge.
So sweetly calm I feel, so lulled to rest,
Though still upon the surging wave. My heart
Pants audibly indeed, yet does not fret.
    Gladly before I die, my future heir
I fain would see. But once, while yet an infant,
I stole a glance at him. How years rush by!
Childhood's best prophecies were written fair
On brow and lip, illumined by the eye:
If that first page lied not, the book is rare.

Enter EUSEBIUS, *bearing a dish.*

EUSEB. Good day, Ignotus, I have longed to see
    you,
Since our return. My noble lord, Euphemian,
Now gives me cause. Accept from him this food,
Prepared for his own table. But, good heavens!
How sadly altered you appear! Art ill?
ALEX. I am but passing well.
EUSEB.   I fear, Ignotus,
That in our absence you have suffered much
From the unruly, ill-bred slaves.
ALEX.   Oh! no.
For it would ill become me to complain,
Who was sent here to practice deeper patience
Than ever hermit in his desert grot.
Its end is near!

EUSEB. What mean you, friend Ignotus?

ALEX. You soon will know. But tell me of this
boy.

EUSEB. Carinus?

ALEX. Yes. Is he a worthy heir
To good Euphemian?

EUSEB. I would almost say
To best Alexius. But yourself shall know him.
For much he longs to hold some converse with
you,
Bred up himself in Asia.

ALEX. Haste to bring him.

EUSEB. [*going.*] I go to seek.

ALEX. [*taking up the dish.*] While I these dainties
bear
To Gannio at the door; he loves them dearly.

[*As he is speaking, enter* URSULUS, *meeting him.* EUSEB. *stops
suddenly at the door on the other side, and looks from a distance unseen.*]

URS. Hallo, sirrah! whither so fast with that nice
dish? Give it up instantly!

ALEX. Willingly, pray accept it from me!

URS. Accept, indeed, what belongs to me! What
right have you, a beggarly intruder, to intercept
what, of right, belongs to the household? I
will not accept, I take it.

6

[*Snatches away the dish, and pushes* ALEX. *rudely, who staggers
backwards on the couch, and rises again faint, standing in the
middle. Just at this moment,* CARINUS *enters, opposite to*
EUSEBIUS, *and starts at seeing this act, but retires to the back
of the stage, and remains unseen behind a pillar.*]

EUSEB. [*rushing forward and seizing the dish.*]
Avaunt, foul harpy! ravenous, impure!
Defiling what thou touchest!

[*He pushes him across the stage, so that he staggers against* PROC-
ULUS *entering. Then puts down the plate.*]

PROC.   How now, slave?
URS. Eusebius, Sir, pushed me against you, after
snatching a dish from me, which I was bearing
from Ignotus to Gannio.
EUSEB. He lies, Sir, foully.
PROC.   Peace, thou forward slave!
EUSEB. No more than thou a slave.
PROC.   Ha! dar'st thou, sirrah!
EUSEB. Sirrah me, sir, no more! I'm free as thou.
PROC. We'll see just now. Come, Ursulus, say on.
URS. I say then that it's all along of that inter-
loper, Ignotus. Since he came into the house,
there has been no peace. We have had nothing
but quarrels on his account. And Eusebius has
always taken his part, in spite of what you bid
us, five blessed years ago.
PROC. Thou sayest true. Like a needle or an

arrow-point imbedded in the flesh, is a stranger that thrusts himself into a house. Wherever it moveth, it causeth irritation and pain.

EUSEB. And pray did *he* intrude himself, or did the master of the house invite, nay press him?

PROC. What care I, so he's here against *my* will?

ALEX. Nay, but I knew not that it was so, Proculus.

PROC. You must have been most stupid, then.

ALEX. How so?

PROC. Could you not see, before you had been here

A single hour, how I had vowed a vow,

That not five more you should remain?

EUSEB. That vow

Proved false as he who made it.

PROC. Silence, slave!

ALEX. Had you but told it, never would Ignotus

Have stood between it and fulfilment.

PROC. Then

Here I renew it. shall it be fulfilled?

ALEX. Surely; to-morrow I go hence.

EUSEB. No; never.

PROC. I take you at your word, Ignotus. Go!

URS. Aye, to the gallows, if you like, false palmer.

PROC. To-morrow, by this hour—

URS. Make yourself scarce.

ALEX. It shall be so.

EUSEB.   I say it shan't.

PROC.   Why not?

EUSEB. 'Twill be a day of joy.

PROC.   Doubly, without him.

EUSEB. 'Twill bring a curse upon the house—

URS.   A blessing!

ALEX. Peace, friends!   Like Jonas, cast me into
    the depths

Of seething ocean, to restore your calm!

But let me reckon with you ere I go.

Ursulus, tell me, wherein have I wronged you?

URS. Why, in merely being here.   You are an
    eyesore to me, a blotch, an excrescence, an ugly
    wart.   Do these things wrong any one?   Yet,
    who can bear them?   Whom does a spider hurt,
    or a house-lizard, or a centipede?   Yet who
    does not loathe and hate them?   [*Savagely.*]
    Who would not gladly set his foot on one of
    them when he sees it, and crush it thus!   [*Stamp-
    ing.*]   Their offence is merely their presence,
    their existence!   And that is yours.

ALEX. [*smiling.*] Well, my existence is beyond
    my reach,

My presence I have promised to relieve you of.

Now, Proculus, with you a parting word.

Be it in peace!

PROC.   Aye, peace eternal!

ALEX. [*mildly.*]   Proculus,
You have not squandered gentleness on me,
Nor lavished kindness, since I entered here.
I speak not to reproach; you did not mean it:
Nor am I worthy of aught better.

EUSEB.   Oh!
Speak not thus, good Ignotus. You have been
Foully misused.

PROC.   Peace, slave, I say again!

ALEX. Forbear, Eusebius; well, I know myself.
  [*Carinus draws nearer, still unnoticed.*]
Friend, [*to Proc.*] have I ever murmured a
  complaint,
E'en to the winds, much less to others' ears?
Have I not bent me enough to your reproaches,
Bowed lowly enough before your scorn, or
  sunk
Not prostrate quite, beneath the sullen blow,
Or stinging buffet of you, or your servants?

PROC. Hold, villain, hold,—

EUSEB.   The "villain" in thy teeth!

ALEX. Eusebius, if you love me, silence! Proculus,
Say if in this I have not so demeaned me
As hath well pleased you, and I'll crave your
  pardon.
If I have not been meek enough and humble,

6*

If I have scandalized some weaker brother,
By haughty bearing, while within this house,
Tell me, that to the very dust I may
Stoop before you and him, and part forgiven.

EUSEB. Nay, 'tis for *him* to ask your pardon.

PROC.   Bah !
You came to act a part, and well have acted !
The sleek and smooth-faced palmer, unrepining
At a snug berth.   Some patience is good pay
For five years' shelter, clothing, food and alms.
Where is the beggar that can't bear a taunt,
Aye, or a blow, for one coin?   But five years'
Living, upon the sweat of others' brows,
Must be a beggar's paradise !

EUSEB.   Shame! shame!

PROC. Aye, shame enough ! that a young sturdy
          vagrant
Should eat the bread of honest, toiling folk.

URS. Honester than himself, I'll warrant you.

PROC. Shame, that he should be sitting all the
          day,
As if at home, within another's house,
Instead of putting out his strength to interest,
And drawing food from his strong, sinewy arm.

URS. Pampered, too, with the best of everything !

PROC. Can I, who bear the burden of this house,
With patience see a lazy parasite

Missing Page

This Ursulus was rudely plundering
Ignotus of the food you sent to him,
And I but rescued it.

Urs.   O foul untruth!
I heard Ignotus say he wished it taken
To Gannio; so I took it.

Euph.   What has this
To do with what I saw?

Proc.   'Tis that these two
Make common cause to worry all your house-
    hold,
Leave it no peace, no rest.   And I must own,
I let my feelings carry me too far,
When you surprised me.

Euph.   And you, then, Ursulus?

Urs. My tender feelings too were wounded, Sir,
He called me harpy!

Euph.   Who?

Urs.   Eusebius.

Euph. Then why revenge yourself upon Ignotus?

Euseb. Give me your ear a moment, Sir.

Proc.   Nay, first
Listen to me, I claim my right.

Euph.   Proceed.

Proc. Ignotus, Sir, did sore provoke me first.
He taunted me with having scorned, ill-used
    him;

After five years of hospitality,
Spoke of himself as of an injured man.
CAR. [*from behind.*] O lying villain!
PROC. [*startled.*]   Did I hear a voice?
EUPH. 'Twas but an echo. Saith he true, Igno-
  tus?
  Speak, friend, and ease my soul. [*Pauses.*]
    You will not say?
EUSEB. I will speak for him. It is a false tale
From first to last, that Proculus hath told.
PROC. 'Tis true, Sir, every word. Speak, Ursulus.
URS. If it's not true, I never spoke the truth.
PROC. See, then, what I assert, Sir, is—
CAR.   A lie!
    [*All start; Proc. and Urs. tremble.*]
EUPH. Methought I heard a sound! It must be
  fancy.
  How shall I judge between such jarring words,
  Such yeas and nays?
PROC.   Why thus, Sir, Ursulus
  And I agree on one side. On the other,
  Eusebius stands alone—
EUSEB.   Come speak, Ignotus.
ALEX. [*to Euph.*] I am not worth disputing thus
  about,
  For so I add affliction to your charity.
  Who am I that should contradict or one

Or the other?   Pray be reconciled—once more
Be friends.

PROC.   You see he bears no testimony,
We therefore stand two witnesses 'gainst—

CAR. [*coming forward.*]   TWO.
I have heard all.

PROC. [*aside.*] 'Twas then his voice we heard,
All is now lost!

CAR.   From first to last—aye all.
Eusebius hath said true—the others false.

PROC. And shall a stripling's word decide the case
Against two old and faithful servants?

CAR.   YES.
Father! or rather master here of all!
Be you our common judge! I know I'm young,
Not witty, nor endowed with brilliant parts,
With ready thought or speech.   One gift alone
From infancy I have possessed and higher
     prized,
And cherish still.—

PROC. [*ironically.*] And pray what is it?

CAR.   TRUTH.
My lips have never lied, nor will, Euphemian.
Brutal in speech and action both have been
To this your holy guest. [*Taking Alexius'
     hand.*]
                    Be thou, Ignotus,

My tutor from henceforth, my guide, my friend;
Teach me but half the virtue I have seen
This hour in thee, reserving to thyself
The bloom so exquisite that made it lovely:—
Be thou to me Alexius. He, if lost,
Be in thee found! So like you are in virtue!
And what are learning, genius, wisdom, save
The gems wherein to set that peerless brilliant?

ALEX. [*moved.*] O dearest child! would I could
    hear thee oft:
To learn and not to teach.

CAR.   But you have promised
    This Proculus, to leave to-morrow.

EUPH.   Is it so?

ALEX. It is, and I must keep my word.

CAR. [*to Euph.*]   Nay, then
    You must command, where I can but entreat.

EUPH. Ignotus, hear a father's supplication;—
                     [*Alexius starts.*
Father to this poor orphan! Stay and bless
This house so long as heaven gives you life.
Promise me this.

ALEX.   Most faithfully I promise.

PROC. [*aside.*] Prevaricator!

ALEX. [*to Proc.*]   And be true to you.

EUPH. How can that be?

ALEX.   To-morrow you shall see.
    Till then be all forgotten, all be peace.

Missing Page

Missing Page

GAN. I was going to say,—a hypocrite. Well, it is not so bad!

BIB. Now, Gannio, that I see you are as staunch as ever, I will tell you of a better thing than poisoning Euphemian.

GAN. What is that?

BIB. Robbing him.—Just listen. How can a man of your spirit sit outside of a house, begging for its scraps, when there are heaps of gold inside, to be had for—

GAN. Hanging, eh?

BIB. Nonsense, man. You may be rich without risk. To-morrow Honorius dines there, and I know that on such an occasion the table is all laid out the night before. A like opportunity may never occur again, in our time. Let me see—the last time was the day when that foolish boy Alexius ran away; just ten years to-morrow. I remember the table well. Such plate! none of your shim-sham silver gilt, but real sterling gold, for centuries in the family. Such candelabra, such urns, and huge dishes, and flagons.

GAN. With such wine in them, eh?

BIB. Not yet. We must keep sober over it, Gannio.

GAN. Of course. [*Puts a bottle slung round him to his mouth.*]

BIB. My turn, if you please. [*Drinks from it.*] But we must have assistance. Do you know of a couple of trustworthy villains, Gannio? two honest scoundrels?

GAN. Aye, do I, two as cunning as foxes, and as bold as lions.

BIB. Perhaps, too, as ferocious as tigers. [*Gan. nods.*] So much the better. What are their names?

GAN. I don't know; but we'll call one of them *First Robber* and 't'other *Second Robber*, as they do in a play.

BIB. Aye, but we are not acting a play, surely?

GAN. No, no, Bibulus, a hanging matter is no play. Now so much for our *pals*. I will secure *them;* next comes how to manage the *plant.*

BIB. We must meet here at dusk, and I will get you with myself into a neglected cellar at the back of the house. All will be busy opening the huge iron chests, unpacking and cleaning and laying out the plate. Towards morning they will all go to rest; and we will quietly walk into the triclinium, fill our sacks—none of your wallets, good big sacks—and walk out by the front door. The only difficulty is where to stow away the plunder.

Gan. I'll manage that. In a back street hard by lives a friend of mine. One sometimes, you know, picks up an odd brooch or ring, that has fallen off a person, and needs a friend to dispose of it.

Bib. Good; he has always the pot boiling, I suppose? But how does he pay?

Gan. Why, to tell the truth, only so so.

Bib. What does he give for wrought gold, for instance?

Gan. For gold he gives the price of old silver.

Bib. Unconscionable villain! How *can* people be so dishonest! And for silver?

Gan. The value of brass.

Bib. Why it is downright robbery! A complete oppression! Then for brass?

Gan. Oh, he would not thank you, even, for any amount of it.

Bib. I suppose he has plenty of his own already.

Gan. Lots. Then all is arranged. I will go and see my friends. At dusk we meet again. [*Kicks aside his wooden bowl.*] There, out of my sight, vile platter—henceforward Gannio disdains all but gold. [*Exeunt severally.*

SCENE IV.—*The Atrium.*

Enter ALEXIUS *and* CARINUS.

CAR. Edessa, then, has been your chief abode,
   During your Eastern pilgrimage. You loved
    it?
ALEX. Dearly; it is a city of much beauty,
   Its houses stately, and its churches gorgeous.
   And then besides it is in truth a place
   Of gentle breeding, and of courtly manners.
   Nor is this all. The East does not possess
   A seat of learning more renowned than that.
CAR. I well remember that, in Syria, youths
   Who panted after knowledge oft would say,
   "I will to famed Edessa, there to study."*
ALEX. Truly, because each nation hath a home
   Within its walls. Syrians, Armenians, Per-
    sians,
   There pass their youth in quest of varied lore.
    From many fountains elsewhere issue rills
   Of letters and of science; some will creep
   Winding along the plain, and dallying
   With flowers of enervating fragrance; some
   Bound sparkling and impetuous from the rock,

*Edessa, the earliest Christian University, had national col-
leges for Eastern nations, at this time.

7*

And threaten rudely delicacy of faith.
But in Edessa these all flow alike
Into one deep yet crystal cistern,
Filled, by King Abgar, with the flood of life
Fresh from its source.*   There they are puri-
    fied,
Filtered, refined ; and issue, each distinct,
Yet all impregnate with celestial lymph.

CAR. How marvellous must be this graceful blend-
    ing
Of the two wisdoms, into one design.
   But say, Ignotus, could a boy like me,
With nought else gifted but *desire* to learn,
There profit gain ?

ALEX.   You measure profit ill.
The vaunt of youth lies not in ready wit,
Shrewdness of thought, or sprightliness of
    speech,—
Torrents in spring that leave dry summer beds,
Trees that yield early, but ill-ripening, fruit.
The grace of youth is in the open brow,
Serene and true ; in blooming cheeks, that blush
Praise to receive, but glow with joy, to give;
In eye that drinks in, flashes not forth, light,

---

* According to primitive tradition, he received Christianity
from its living Founder.

Fixed on the teacher's lips, as hope's on heaven;
In the heart docile, unambitious, steadfast.—
A youth with these may bind a smaller sheaf,
But every ear contains a solid grain,
Which heaven's sun and dew have swelled and
    ripened—
Bread of the present life, seed of the next.*

CAR. It cheers me, so to hear you talk, Ignotus.
But in my heart deep lies a secret thought
To man yet unrevealed. Your words so sweet
Would charm it from its nest—

ALEX.   Perhaps unfledged.

CAR. Yet soon must it have wings. Tell me, Ig-
    notus,
Can it be wrong in one so weak as I,
To fly at lofty heights, sublimest aims?

---

* The following was the text used, at the performance of the Drama, at the Jubilee.

CAR. It cheers my heart to hear you talk, Ignotus.
But tell me more: is there among those homes
Of solid learning one which you prefer?

ALEX. Where all are excellent, 'tis hard to choose.
Affection only may decide.

CAR.   E'en this
From you might guide selection.

ALEX. [*surprised.*] What! is ambition. creeping
   in already,
   To torture your young heart? So needless, too!
   For yours are wealth, nobility, command
   O'er a vast appanage.
CAR.   Nay, judge me not
   So meanly, Ignotus; nigher far I soar.
ALEX. Higher than Rome's first Senator? [*With
   emotion.*] What! child,
   O no! it cannot be!—You cannot dream
   To match your flight against the Roman Eagle's,
   Snatch the world's sceptre, and usurp a purple
   Then surely doubly dyed. O no, Carinus,
           [*Affectionately.*]

ALEX.   Listen then.
   I best remember one of large dimensions,
   Furnished with all its purpose could demand,
   A noble library, a stately hall,
   Art-bedecked cloisters, many-chapelled church.
   I often lingered by its walls to hear
   Now sacred chaunts, now shouts of youthful
       glee.
CAR. How is it called, Ignotus?
ALEX.   Near its gates
   A lordly yew once spread its boughs; as yet,

Such hideous fancies darken not your soul.
But should their distant pest-cloud but approach,
Fly from its baleful shadow as from death!
CAR. O, dear Ignotus, this would be to fall,
With broken pinion, lower; not to rise.
Earth's gifts while scorning, can I love its
crimes?
ALEX. Then solve me your enigma, dearest child.
CAR. A nobler name than "Cæsar" or "Augus-
tus"
I covet: such commands I long to issue
As angels execute, and demons dread:
To wear no purple, but what *once* He wore—
The King that ruled o'er Pilate's mocking
court:

Unplumed by time, its hollow trunk there
stands,
And gives it name.*
CAR. Proceed, good friend.
ALEX. It chanced,
As I Edessa left, that I did pass
Before its porch, and saw unusual stir,
Great preparations for a festive day.
They bid me gently, and I entered in.—

* *Ushaw*, supposed to have thus received its name.

To stand before an altar, not a throne,
Bearing not the world's lordship, but its Lord!

ALEX. [*tenderly.*] O, loved Carinus, how my fears
    have wronged you!
May heaven's bright blessing beam on your re-
    solve;
May choicest grace bedew its tender roots,
Till it grow up to ripeness. But, my child,
Have you weighed well its sequences, condi-
    tions,
Its difficulties, sacrifices, loss?
Euphemian binds to you, as its first link,
The chain of long succession to his name;—
While you would close it.

It was my palmer's privilege. They said
That day they kept their JUBILEE.

CAR.   What meant they?

ALEX. 'Twas the completion of just fifty years
Since they had there abode.

CAR.   A happy day,
And joyful, must that jubilee have been!

ALEX. Aye, had you seen those youths' bright
    faces, heard
Their ringing cheers, their gladsome minstrelsy,
Tasted their bounteous banquet, witnessed

CAR.   But how gloriously!
   The priest, like the apostle, *ends* his line,
   However proud its nobleness, more nobly;
   As the sun's furnace yields at eve its gold.
ALEX. How tell Euphemian this?
CAR.   There is my trial.
   And yet to-morrow it must needs be told.
   Will you not help me? [*Caressingly.*]
ALEX. [*looking upwards, and thoughtfully.*] Yes,
      dear boy, I will.
   So noble is your thought, so sweetly told:
   So dovelike is your nestling, yet beyond
   The eaglet I had deemed it, that if e'en
   It needed for its growth my heart's best blood,

   The sacred drama they so well performed,
   In honor of the day, you, though a stranger,
   Would have pronounced it joyful, happy day!
CAR. Indeed I would! and were there strangers
      there?
ALEX. Yes; many whom kind courtesy had
      brought.
   But there were others whom affection drew,
   Or duty even; for they called that house
   Their mother.   Some were venerable prelates,
   And many, holy priests, who once had walked

There, like the pelican, I'd feed it willingly,
Till thence you drew it forth.
CAR.   O speak not so;
  To-morrow you shall help me to disclose
  My so long burrowing purpose. [*Hesitating.*]
      And perhaps
  You then will tell me your own history.
  Ignotus—pardon—you are not what men
  Take you for.   'Neath that coarse dress, and in
      that
  Spare form, those features wan, there lurks a
      spark
  Of noble nature, and of brilliant fire.
  Oh! tell me who you are!

  Along those cloisters, book in hand, to con
  Their youthful lessons; there were many, too,
  Who thence had gone to battle with the world;
  And now returned, to thank the very walls
  Whence they had plucked their arms. Glad-
      ness prevailed,
  And mutual gratulation.   All felt bound
  In one community of grateful love.
CAR. But surely, few could measure back that
      term
  Of half a century?

ALEX.   Yes, yes, to-morrow!
CAR. To-morrow! Everything on that dark day!
  It looks to me like a storm-laden cloud,
  Embosoming blight, fever, dark dismay.
  And yet athwart it darts one precious beam
  Of glory, shooting from the deepest hue.
  It bears your name, Ignotus, and it shines
  Upon my future way.

ALEX.   Alas! but few.
  And in the house one only. In the midst
  Of all he sate, uniting old and young,
  Friends of his youth, disciples of his age;
  So that he smiled on all, and made all smile.
  His life the chain, which, threading one by one
  The circlets of past fifty years, joined them
  Into one generation. Many hung
  From ring or link;—alone he held both ends.
    So many had he led on wisdom's path,
  So many had sustained up virtue's steep,
  That by consent they called him all—"the Doc-
      tor,"
  Aye, "the old Doctor," was their name of love.*
CAR. O, dear Ignotus, you have made me envious
  Of others' happiness—but you seem weary.

*The Rt. Rev. Mgr. Newsham, President of St. Cuthbert's
College.

  3

ALEX. [*deeply affected.*] Blest be its omen!
But you are wanted—so farewell, my child,
Farewell—who knows? Yes, yes, we meet again!
CAR. Farewell until that terrible to-morrow!
ALEX. [*thoughtfully and tenderly.*] 'Twill not be
terrible when next we meet.
When our eyes glass themselves in one another's,
Tears will have been wiped from them; mourn-
ing none,
Nor pain, nor sigh, will be; first things are passed.
CAR. Farewell; I'll try to dream, then, of that
bright to-morrow!   [*Exeunt.*

ALEX. I should have been much more, except for
you.
CAR. How so?
ALEX.   Because nought is so sweet to me
As to converse with fresh ingenuous youth,
And guide its opening impulses.   I fear,
My child, that you are wanted; till to-morrow
Farewell!
CAR.   That terrible to-morrow!   But,
Ignotus, talk to me again and soon,
To-night my dreams shall bear me to Edessa.
ALEX. May they be omens of a true event!
You, who are young, oh, may you live to see
A second, not a brighter, Jubilee!   [*Exeunt.*

SCENE V.--*The same*

Night. The stage darkened

Enter from the house-side, BIBULUS, GANNIO, *and two robbers. Each is muffled up, and carries a sack heavily loaded; the two robbers have knives or daggers in their girdles. They grope one after another,* BIBULUS *leading.*

BIB. This way, masters, this way, we are now just at the door.

1ST ROB. Which way?

BIB. Why this way.

2D ROB. But which *is* this way?

BIB. Follow me, you—

1ST ROB. Come, no sauce—where *are* you?

BIB. Follow your nose, then, straight across the court.

[*At length they meet in the middle.*]

Here we are at last altogether. Now take hold of one another, and follow me.

[*As they do so, a glimmer of light appears from* ALEXIUS'S *cell. They turn round, and see him kneeling with his arms extended. They stand in attitudes of amazement, two on each side; and as the scene proceeds, one by one lay down their sacks, stupified and overawed. The light goes on increasing, till it reaches, before the chorus, its utmost brightness.*]

ALEX. Ye blessed spirits, watch over this house, Defend its goods and inmates from the prowler;

And if mine own long-wished-for hour draw
    nigh,
Oh, let me hear once more your minstrelsy.

CHORUS OF UNSEEN SPIRITS.

Angels watch, aloft to bear,
Pilgrim youth! thy parting prayer.
    Into night's dark veil is weaving
      Golden threads the coming sun;
    Earth's cold gloom behind thee leaving,
      Haste thy course of light to run.
On our bosoms sunk to rest,
Wake among thy kindred Blest!

ALEX. [*starting up.*] I come, I come, I come;—
    oh! tarry for me.

[*The robbers run away, out of the house—Day breaking.*]

ALEX. [*recovering from his trance, roused by the
    noise.*]
    What means all this—what have we here?
      Ha! thieves!
    'Tis well I watched; what treasures they have
      seized!
    The door must be made fast; [*shuts and bolts it.*]
      and until day
    Has roused the slumbering family, this spoil

Will be securer here! [*Puts the sacks into his
    cell and shuts it.*]
            Well, thanks to heaven!
My poor last will and testament is written.
    [*Looks at a scroll, and puts it back into his
    bosom.*]
So I am ready. [*A great noise of trampling and
    calling out from the house.*]
            Ah! the theft's discovered.

Enter PROCULUS, *and all the servants, in great confusion and
    with much noise.*

URS. They must have got out this way. The
    back door is closed, and I have been at it these
    two hours.
PROC. Ah! Ignotus. You too are up betimes;
    have you seen any robbers pass this way?
ALEX. No, but I heard them running off.
DAV. [*picking up a spoon.*] Here is proof that
    they have passed through this!
PROC. [*who has been to the door.*] Aye, and more-
    over, the front door is bolted and barred; so,
    courage, boys! the robber is still in the house.
    He shan't escape.
VER. [*looking into the cell.*] Eureka! eureka!
    Here's the plunder, lads; here's the magpie's
    nest! Look! look!

8*

[*They draw out the sacks, and surround* ALEXIUS, *in menacing attitudes, and with angry gestures.*]

DAV. So you didn't see the robbers, eh? Good reason why: you had never no looking-glass in your room.

VER. Perhaps if you had had your slippers on, you wouldn't have *heard* them either.

PROC. Well, I think this time, my good pilgrim, you will not wind yourself so easily out of it: [*Aside*] and that forward boy is not here to help you.

Enter EUPHEMIAN *and* EUSEBIUS.

EUPH. How now, my men? It is strange that the very day on which my house is to be most highly honored, and I wished it to be the most orderly and peaceful, should commence with absolute tumult, as if the place were possessed by evil spirits.

PROC. One at least, Sir, we have found; but I hope we shall be able to lay him effectually this time. [*Pointing to Alexius, who is faint and in pain.*]

EUPH. What! again, and so soon after my proclaiming a truce to your quarrels till after the festivities of to-day, are you insulting and assailing the good man?

PROC. The good man indeed! the thief, the robber of your house. [*Showing the sacks.*]

EUPH. Good heavens! What means this?

PROC. It means neither more nor less than that
during the night the most valuable portion of
your plate, laid out for the imperial banquet,
has been carried off, that the doors are all fast-
ened inside, and that we have found it all in
Ignotus' room.

EUSEB. Do not believe so clumsy a tale, Sir. Depend upon it, this is only a conspiracy got up
against him.

URS. We are all witnesses to the truth.

ALL. Yes, Sir, all of us.

EUPH. Surely, Ignotus, this cannot be true?
And yet the evidence seems strong against you.
This time you *must* explain. [*Pauses.*] What,
 not a syllable?

EUSEB. O dear Ignotus, one word will suffice.
Your *no* will answer all their accusations.

ALEX. And yet I may not speak it. [*Aside to
Euseb.*]
        Good Eusebius,
My lips are sealed.

EUSEB. Oh, not by guilt, just heaven?

ALEX. No: by example, too sublime to name.

EUPH. Ignotus, I implore you, speak.—Still silent?

Speak, or I must believe your guilt.—No an-
    swer?
This silence doth condemn you,—wretched
    man—[*sorrowfully and indignantly.*]
    Have I then ta'en a viper to my bosom,
Whom worthy I had deemed to be a son?
A faithless robber for a holy man?
And have five years of seeming piety,
Of feigned austerity, and sham religion,
Been but a hypocrite's deep preparation
For vilest treachery, and meanest crime?
Who will believe again in human virtue,
If this be true?

ALEX.   Oh, spare me! mercy! pity!

EUPH. Aye, pity me, who have been cozened so!
    Ignotus, had you wanted gold, and told me,
    You should have had it, in its choicest forms.
    I loved you well, and thought I owed you much!
    Now you have shamed yourself, alas! and me;
    Before my servants and my child, have made
    Virtue a byword, godliness a scorn.

ALEX. [*staggering forward.*] Believe it not; but,
    oh! I am so faint,
    I cannot speak.

EUPH.   Alas! remorse, I fear,
    Chokes up your utterance, and saps your
    strength.

Better confess your guilt by one short word,
And seek forgiveness!

ALEX. [*looking about, distracted.*] Oh! where is
that boy?

EUPH. Never shall you set eye on him again,
To blight his virtue by its basilisk gaze.
Go, go, Ignotus, go in peace—forever.

ALEX. [*endeavoring to approach, and kneel before
him.*]
Oh! spurn me not; by all that is most dear
Still to your heart; by your poor son, long lost;
By him who will this day replace him, I
Conjure you, hear me.

EUPH.   No, Ignotus, no! [*Motioning
him back.*]
Fly from my sight, thine hour to go hath
knelled.

ALEX. Ah! now I know 'tis true; Angels, I come!
From other hands I well could stand a *blow*,
The wave of *that* is death.   It fills my cup—
To die a thief reputed in that heart,
Where, upon earth, alone I cared for love!
Farewell!

[*He sinks back into* EUSEBIUS'S *arms, and is laid on a couch,
raised so as to face the audience.   His right hand hangs by his
side, his left is close pressed on his bosom.*]

EUPH. Let him lie there to gather strength,
Then give him means to go.

Euseb.   Sir, 'tis too late,
    His last is breathed on earth.
Euph.   Oh! say not so!
    'Twould be an end too horrible; a robber's
    Invoking Angels, unrepented, too!

Enter CARINUS.

Car. What hath occurred so early to disturb you?
Euseb. See here, my boy, your friend Ignotus
        dead!
Car. Impossible! Awake, Ignotus, rise—
                                    [*Alarmed.*
    It cannot be! what can have killed him?
Proc.   Conscience!
Car. What does that mean?
Proc.   Remorse!
Dav.   He died a thief.
Ver. Just to escape a hanging.
Car.   I'm bewildered!
    No, no, his spirit can't be fled. He'll keep
    His promise to me, to remain with me. [*Kneel-
        ing and taking his hand in both his.*]
    Will you not speak to your new pupil? Press
    His hand at least. Yours is yet warm! Oh
        give
    One token that you know him! Ah me! I fear
        [*Bursting into grief.*]

It is too true; some sudden cause hath driven
His soul to an abode more worthy of it.
If so, before high heaven, I protest
Against it loudly, and declare him guiltless.

EUPH. [*roused out of deep sorrow, passionately.*]
Let go that hand, Carinus, lest its touch
Pollute you! 'tis a robber's child!

CAR. [*looking up, astonished.*] A robber's?

EUPH. Aye, a blasphemer's, too!

CAR.   Blasphemer's?

EUPH. One who by his hypocrisy would nigh
Make us henceforth forswear all virtue!

CAR.   How, Sir?
What can this mean? Do you, then, join your
    slaves
In hateful condemnation of your friend?

EUPH. Oh, yes, at last plain evidence of guilt
Hath flashed upon me.

CAR.   Though 'twere like the sun,
I would deny its ray.

EUPH. [*pulling him away.*] Come, leave that bier
To its own load of guilt.

CAR.   What guilt?

EUPH.   First, theft,
Basest in kind; and after 'twas committed,
And rank remorse, or heaven's unseen bolt,
Had felled the culprit, he, without repentance,
Commended him to Angels' hands.

CAR.   Enough!
No hardened villain could have done as much!
Still less a gentle, saintly youth like him!
One hour of converse with him yesterday,
Made me well know him!   I dare to proclaim
His innocence, and challenge all to proof
Of any guilt in dear Ignotus.
EUPH.   Rash
And foolish boy, I needs must call you, now.
Last night this house was robbed of precious
    plate,
And there it lies! [*Pointing to the sacks.*]
CAR.   But pray, where was it found?
PROC. Within his cell.
CAR. [*thoughtful and abstracted.*] And so was
    Joseph's cup
Found in the sack of Benjamin—yet, still,
He was no thief! others may there have left it.
EUPH. This is unreasonable—e'en in a child.
The door was closed and bolted from inside,
No one can have escaped.
CAR. [*after a moment's pause.*] Eusebius, Proculus,
Haste to the door; fresh sand was strewn before it
For the imperial visit yester-eve.
A morning shower hath crisped its surface; see
If footsteps have yet pressed it. [*They go and
    return.*]

EUSEB. Heaven bless thee, gifted boy! the prints
    are clear,
  Of two men to the right, two to the left,
  Fleeing from off the very door step.
PROC.   Four,
  No doubt, have passed the threshold.
CAR.   And just four
  Are these thieves' packages.
EUSEB.   O noble youth!
  What instinct have the pure to find the truth!

[*A loud knocking at the door; it is opened. Enter an officer,
dragging in* BIBULUS *and* GANNIO, *handcuffed.*]

OFFICER. Hath anything happened amiss in your
  house, my lord? These two men were seen to
  run out of it, and, after a hot pursuit, have been
  captured. Two others took another direction,
  and I fear have escaped. [*He throws off their
  hats.*]
SEVERAL. Bibulus, I declare!
OTHERS. Gannio, upon my word!
BIB. [*kneeling.*] Good Sir, once more forgive me!
EUPH. Surely I am bewitched! What means all
  this?
BIB. Last night, we two—
GAN.   Indeed, Sir, he induced me
  To join in robbing you, with two companions.

9

EUPH. Speak, one or other, but go on.

BIB. [*rising.*]   We filled—
    Aye, there they are—four sacks with plate. Thus
        far,
    We had in safety reached.—

EUPH.   Well, who then stopped you?

BIB. He who once saved your life, now saved
    your house.

EUPH. How so? What did he? Speak! my
    heart will break!

BIB. We heard him pray that Angels would pro-
    tect it;
    Then shone a glory round him like the sun,
    While unseen spirits in a heavenly strain
    Welcomed him to them. Scared, we fled away,
    As Roman soldiers before Easter's ray.

EUPH. Oh! wretched man I am! This day I
    hoped
    Would bring joy, honor, glory to my house,
    Yet hath it bred more grief and anguish here
    Than any other anniversary.
    Oh! shame to have thus spurned the innocent,
    Nay, almost cursed him! seen him die, un-
        moved,
    Loaded his corse with ignominy! Oh! blind-
        ness,
    Not to have learnt, after five years' experience,

What one day taught this child, his depth of
   virtue!
My life indeed must now be spent in weeping
Over such guilt!
            But, Proculus, haste, tell,
As best you can, the Emperor my grief,
And beg indulgence till a brighter day!
PROC. Stay; for here comes a royal chamberlain.

Enter CHAMBERLAIN.

CHAMB. Noble Euphemian, I come from Hono-
   rius;
He follows shortly.
EUPH.   We are not prepared
Thus early.   Why this haste?
CHAMB.   Have you not heard,
That through the churches of the entire city,
A voice has clearly rung, " Haste to the Aven-
   tine,
A saint hath died there!"   Crowds are flocking
   hither
By every avenue.   The Emperor
And Pontiff Innocent have sent me forward
To ascertain the spot; for no one knows
Where any saint hath lived, and may have died.
EUPH. Oh! viler still am I!   A virtuous man,
Methought I had misjudged, yet 'tis a saint

I have held in my house five years, nor known
      him!
And at his death I have reviled him!   Go,
Pray my good lords, the Emperor and Pope,
Not to approach the house of one so sinful
As I have been, till tears have washed my guilt.
CAR. Oh! weep not, father, comfort soon will
      come.
These, your good princes, may be sent to bear it.
There was a purpose in this great concealment,
A mystery of virtue unrevealed,
Buried in this deep heart:—[*Touches Alexius'
      breast.*]
Ha! and is this its epitaph?   [*Draws a scroll
      from the hand on the bosom.   All look
      amazed.*]
                              What's here?

[*Opens the scroll, looks at it, shrieks as he lets it fall, and throws
   himself in passionate grief across the bier.   EUSEBIUS picks up
   the scroll and gives it to EUPHEMIAN, who looks at it, drops it,
   and buries his face in his hands, moaning.*]

EUPH. O woe is me! deeper my anguish still!
Keener my shame, blacker my crime!   Alas!
That I should not have known thee, not dis-
      covered!
That I should have been dead to every throb
Of a paternal heart, deaf to its cries!

Nay, that I should have overlooked the yearn-
ings
Of thy true filial love, to be reclaimed—
(So many instances I now remember)—
Looks to me like a spell cast over me.
But read, Eusebius, read my final sentence.

EUSEB. [*who has taken up the scroll, reads amidst
profound silence and signs of amazement.*]

"I am Alexius, son of the Senator Euphemian. A supreme command sent me away from
my father's house, to wander as a pilgrim for
five years. My time was chiefly passed at
Edessa. After that period, I was similarly
commanded to return, and die in the place
where I was born. My father's charity has
supported me till this my last day.

"I keep my promises to all. Proculus, I
depart hence forever. Carinus, child of my
heart, I remain with you to guide you still,
though unseen.

"My father! mourn not for me; you have
secured for me greater happiness than this world
can give. Be hospitable ever to the stranger:
be charitable to the poor. The heir of your
house is found again, as he has often promised
you. But as you decided, *he* should to-day

9*

make the award between your servants, regard-
ing the pilgrim Ignotus, he hereby pronounces
in favor of universal pardon, forgetfulness, and
reconciliation.

"ALEXIUS."

PROC. Let me be foremost, Sir, to claim this par-
    don,
  As in offending I have been most forward.
  Deeply I grieve my past injustices.
ALL. So do we all.
BIB. *and* GAN. And we our base attempt.
EUPH. All I forgive—but who will pardon me?
  Far in the depths of some Egyptian desert
  Must be my shame and sorrow buried. There
  Tears of repentance may blot out my guilt.
  [*Kneeling by the couch and seizing Alexius'
    hand.*]
    Ah! now I recognize those placid features
  In thee, my son, by which I should have known
    thee!
  Here is thy noble brow, serene in grief,
  Here are thy truthful lips, smiling in death,
  Oh that thine eyes would open;—yet their
    lids
  Can scarce o'ercloud the azure of their orbs!
    [*Rising passionately.*]

How blinded I have been! Oh! who will draw me
From the abyss of my despair?

CAR. [*clinging to Euph.*]   I will.
Remember, father, 'tis in ignorance,
And in obedience to a higher will,
That you have acted. What to you brings sorrow,
Gives him renown on earth, in heaven glory.

EUPH. And what is that?

CAR.   Why, to have meekly died
Under false censure of the kindest judge.
What Isaac would have been, had Abram's knife
Cleft his unmurmuring breast,—that is Alexius.
Nay, more; he could not be the saint he is,
Had he not passed that ' *lamma sabachthani* "
'Tis the sublimest martyrdom of soul.

EUPH. Child, thou hast comforted me! [*To the Chamberlain.*] Go, tell the princes
Who wield the keys and sceptre of both worlds,
That here reposes one in each most great.
Myself and my young heir await them.

                        [*Exit Chamb.*

CAR.   Father,
I pray you speak not so. [*Pointing to Alex.*]
There is your heir,

Returned to claim his own, and keep his promise.
All here is his, and he departs no more.
EUPH. How shall this be?
CAR.   You have no other heir,
I will be none.   Heaven has called him saint;
This is his tomb, his shrine, his temple; here
Must rise a stately church, with ample cloisters,
To lodge the pilgrim; your estates endow it;
You be its faithful steward.
EUPH.   And Carinus?
CAR. Will be its priest.   Till age and law permit,
He'll seek Edessa.   In (its yew-named)* college,
Learning with virtue will make years glide
     quick.
His diligence shall run a race with yours,
So nicely matched, that both of you shall win.
What time the sacred dome shall have been
     built,
Its priest from secret study will emerge.
(For silent toil is youth's best husbandry.)
Here he will toil in his sublime vocation,
Console the sorrowing, rejoice the poor;
The body's ills relieve, but cure the soul's,
And wing it for the flight beyond all pain.
Then when the work and griefs of day are ended,

* *Or* (some fair-famed.)

He'll sit him down beside his cousin's tomb,
To meditate upon his hidden worth,
Inglorious virtues, and unhonored grace,
His humble life, and ignominious end,—
Yet saintly glory!

EUPH.   Oh! Carinus, stay,
The myst'ry now I read of this great day;
Which to my house, through ways by us least
    thought,
More glory, than all earth's renown, has brought.
I read its *lesson*, too, so high and true,—
By him well taught—so be it learnt by you:
"None in the Church's golden diadem
Can shine, that is not long, a hidden gem."

www.ingramcontent.com/pod-product-compliance
Lightning Source LLC
Chambersburg PA
CBHW022356020726
47500CB00002B/298